## About the Author

Susan Price won the Carnegie Medal for *Ghost Drum* in 1987 and was shortlisted again in 1994 for *Head and Tales*. She writes: 'I was born in a slum in Oldbury, West Midlands – no bathroom or running water inside; an outside lavatory shared with several other households; and cockroaches and mice. But we got a council house when I was four, and moved about a mile away, nearer to Dudley, where I still live.

I have a pet, a little grey tabby cat with white patches. She has beautiful pale green eyes, with a black line round them, as if she is wearing mascara. I like sharing my house with another kind of animal. I always have to share my chair with her. Tig's usually curled up somewhere near me while I'm writing.'

*Also published by Hodder Children's Books*

Blackthorn, Whitethorn
*Rachel Anderson*

The Fated Sky
Chance of Safety
*Henrietta Branford*

Burning Issy
*Melvyn Burgess*

Brother Cat, Brother Man
*Zoe Halliday*

The Climb
*Libby Hathorn*

Earthfasts
Cradlefasts
*William Mayne*

Foundling
Escape
*June Oldham*

Mr Tucket
*Gary Paulsen*

Boy In Darkness
*Mervyn Peake*

Hauntings
Nightcomers
*Susan Price*

Waterbound
Secret Songs
*Jane Stemp*

# The Story Collector

Susan Price

*Hodder*
*Children's*
*Books*

a division of Hodder Headline plc

# Contents

# Contents

# One

## Elsie's Story

'Elsie, do you know any other stories?'

Elsie was kneeling before the fire, adding coal to the flames. She looked over her shoulder. 'Stories, Master?'

'Stories. You were telling one in the kitchen the other day, about a woman and the Devil.'

'Oh, that was only what people say, Master.'

'But do you know any other stories?'

Elsie stopped putting coal on the fire, and replaced the fire-tongs. Resting her hands on her knees as she knelt, she said, 'Oh I know a lot of stories – when I can think of 'em. You can't always think of 'em right when you want to, Master.'

'Tell me another.'

Elsie giggled. 'I can't think.' She began to get up. 'You don't want to hear 'em anyway, Master.'

'But I do. I've been thinking that I might write them down.'

Elsie stared. 'Why would you want to do that, Master?'

'So that other people can read them, Elsie – people who

aren't lucky enough to have your acquaintance.'

Elsie, standing by the fire, still stared. 'Folk who can read don't want to read my stories, Master.'

'But they do, my dear, I assure you. I enjoyed your little story about the Devil immensely. Besides, writing them down would give me something to do. I'm sadly in need of something to do since my son took over the Works.'

'But that story, Master, that story about the Devil – that wasn't a story. That happened. My Gran said so.'

'Does your Grandmother tell you a lot of stories?'

Elsie put her head on one side. 'Some. I know one about a shillin', Master.'

'Oh!' The Master turned sideways on his chair, leaning on the table beside him. 'Elsie, my dear, why don't you sit yourself down at the table, and I shall pour you a small glass of my sweet sherry—'

'Oh, Master—'

'Only a little drop – and then you shall tell me the story of the shilling.'

'But Master – kind of you, Master, but I've work to do—'

'It can wait a little while, surely?'

'But Master, I can't go to bed until I get it done, and it takes ages, washing all the crocks and—'

'Oh. Oh, well, I shall have a word with cook, and tell her that you were helping me with my little collection. I'm sure we'll be able to arrange for you to get your beauty sleep.'

Elsie wasn't so sure, but the pretty golden brown of the

sherry that Mr Grimsby poured into the pretty little glass fascinated her. And it would be so much nicer to stay in this warm room, that smelt pleasantly of the polish used on the table, chairs and bookshelves, and of the leather bindings of the books, than to go back to the kitchens, where she would stand at the sink and wash greasy plates and pots, while it got darker, and later, and the fire went out, and her feet grew icy on the stone floor, and her back ached, and her eyes bleared. Even if she had to pay for this pleasant time with long hours of kitchen work later, it would be worth it. So she thought then.

'Do sit down, my dear.'

Elsie, with a thrill, sat on one of the big polished chairs, and picked up the fragile little glass. As she lifted it, a reflection of it moved in the deep polish of the table-top. The sherry was sweet and strong and made her shudder pleasurably. Mr Grimsby was smiling at her across the table, and she smiled back.

'Now, you tell me the story, my dear, and I shall listen very carefully, and after you've gone I shall write it down. Perhaps tomorrow I'll read it to you, and you can tell me if I have it right?'

'That would be nice, Master.'

Mr. Grimsby sat back in his chair and lifted his own glass. 'Do begin.'

'Well, Master, it was like this,' Elsie said. 'Me Gran was coming home one day, across the fields. There's this little stile by hawthorn hedge, and as her come up to the stile her hears somebody singing. Well, her looks about, and her looks about and all round, but her couldn't see nobody. Nobody in sight. But there's this singing:

"*Over the hills and far away!*"

'So me Gran thinks it's somebody behind the hawthorn hedge, singing, and her calls out, "That's a good song!"

> "*O'er the hills and o'er the main,*
> *Through Flanders, Portugal and Spain*
> *O'er the hills and a long way off –*
> *The wind'll blow your top-knot off!*"

'But nobody answers, and the singing goes on and on.

'Her come closer to the stile, and her could hear a sort of tapping and ringing along with the singing, like metal being tapped on stone. But with the music. And still her can't see nobody. Funny, her thinks.

'Anyroad her starts to climb over the stile – and down by the side of the stile there was a flat stone – a thrush's anvil, y'know, with all broken snails' shells around it, and all silver with snail juices, and grass growing thick round it. And as my Gran looks down, her sees, on this stone, a shilling. There's a bright little shilling on the stone, standing up on edge, and this shilling is dancing and singing to itself. And that's what's making the ringing and tapping, and that's where the singing's coming from.

> "*There's King's shilling on the drum*

4

'Me Gran thinks, "A shilling! That'll help keep the wolf away!" So her picked up the shilling and put it in her apron pocket and went on home.

'The shilling went all quiet in her pocket. Stopped dancing. Stopped singing. It was just like a proper shilling – for a bit.

'Well, me Gran got home and her went in and my aunts and uncles was there – when they were little, you know. And her said, "Look what I got," and her put the shilling on the table.

'And the shilling stood up on its edge and it started to dance and sing:

> *"Tom, Tom, was a piper's son*
> *He stole a pig and away he run—"*

'Only it was dancing on wood now, so it made a little rapping noise. And all the little uns come round the table, and they was watching the shilling and laughing—

'Only the shilling starts dancing harder and singing louder. It hopped and jumped on the table, and it sung louder and louder, and the little uns and me Gran started putting their hands over their ears and backing away—

'Only harder and harder the shilling taps on the table, until the table started to split. And louder and louder it starts to sing, until all the pots and pans started to rattle –

5

and then the table's thumping on the flags – and then the walls am shaking! – and plaster started to fall – and me Gran thought the house was coming down. So her grabs the shilling and her—

'—throws it out the door! Throws it as hard and as far as her can. And then her sits down – *whoomf!* – on a chair and catches her breath, and her says to little uns, 'Stop blarting; it's gone, it's gone.'

'So they stopped crying. And they thought everything was all right. "Easy come, easy go," says me Gran. "Lost a shilling, but at least we still got a house."

'But the shilling come back. It woke 'em up the next morning, dancing and singing on the table. And the table was splintering, and the plaster was coming off the walls, and you couldn't hear yourself shout. And the neighbours was standing outside, watching the walls wobble and the window shake in the frames, and saying, "What's going on, what's going on?"

'Me Gran gets up and her says to the shilling, "What do you want, little shilling? Tell me what you want."

'But the shilling just kept singing:

> "*O'er the hills and o'er the main,*
> *To England's sweet green shore again*—"

' "Do you want some milk?" says me Gran, and her sends me auntie running to fetch a jug of milk, and when her got back, they put the jug of milk on the table and me Gran says, "There you am, little shilling – it's all yourn."

'But the shilling just knocked itself against the jug and smashed it, and all the milk run over the table and on to the floor. And the shilling splashed in the milk and sung and sung – and the hammering was so loud, folk had to hold their heads together with their hands. All the walls was shaking. Tiles was coming off the roof. The house was going to fall down!

'So me Gran grabs the shilling again and her went to the door and her says to the crowd outside, "Who wants this, who wants this?" But nobody would have it – well, would you? But somebody says, "Take it to church and put it on the altar."

'Well, me Gran thought that was a good idea, so her run down into the town with the shilling in her hand, and her went to Top Church – you know Top Church, Master, the big un right at the top of the hill? With the big tower? Well, me Gran thought it was the biggest church, so it would be the strongest. And her went in, and it was quiet and cold and dark and nobody was about. And her went up the aisle, and right up to the altar, right up to it, and her put the shilling on the altar with the candlesticks. And it didn't dance and sing there, oh no!

'So me Gran thought her'd fixed it, and her went back through the town and climbs the hill back to her house – and her could see the crowd still outside, and as her got closer, her could see the walls shaking – and her could see the chimney had been shook down – and her could see all the glass from the windows smashed out – and her could hear the hammering and singing from inside and her thought, "Oh no."

> *"Over the hills and a great way off*
> *The wind'll blow your head right off!"*

'And when her got into the house, there was the shilling, dancing and singing on the table. And me Gran sits in a chair and says, "What does it want, what does it want? Oh, it'll just have to shake the house down, I don't know what it wants."

'Then me Mom says – me Mom was just a little girl then – me Mom says, "Shall I take it back where it come from?"

'And me Gran says, "Ar, take it back where it come from. We shall have a few minutes' peace anyroad."

'So me Mom catched the shilling – it took a bit of doing – and her run out the house and down to the fields until her come to the stile by the hawthorn hedge, and the flat stone where the thrushes dropped their snails. And her put the shilling down on the stone, and the little shilling started to hop and skip on the stone and to sing:

> *"O'er the hills and o'er the main,*
> *To England's sweet green shore again—"*

'And it was just singing quiet, to itself. And me Mom run home, and the shilling wasn't there. And it didn't come back. And they was glad enough just for that – that the shilling left 'em in peace – but the next morning me Gran found a gold sovereign in her shoe! Just an ordinary, quiet gold sovereign – it never moved or sung nothing – but me Gran made good use of it! And her said it was give her by the shilling, for putting it back where her found it.

'And whenever me Gran passed that stile after that, and her heard singing, her just kept going and didn't even look. And you, Master – it's all right to pick up any old coin that just lies there – but if ever you come across a little shilling dancing and singing to itself, just you leave it be, and let it sing. Don't you try and take it away, no matter how much you need the money, 'cos you know what'll happen now!'

'But surely,' said Mr Grimsby, 'the thing to do would be to take the shilling home for a while, and then put it back where I found it – and then I would find a sovereign in my shoe!'

'Oh no, Master! The shilling would know! There'd be ashes and trash in your shoe!'

'Oh! Then thank you for the warning, Elsie. I shall try no tricks with dancing shillings.' He took some change from his pocket, shuffled a shilling from it and placed it on the polished table before him. He peered at it. 'I shall respect shillings more now – and I don't think I can do better than hand this little rascal over to you for safe-keeping.' And he reached over the table and dropped the shilling into Elsie's hand.

'Thank you, Master!'

'A pleasure, my dear girl. Tell me – you say your grandmother told you this story?'

'Ar, Master. But it happened, Master, it really happened.'

'Does she know a lot of stories, your grandmother?'

'Hundreds and hundreds, Master.'

'Do you think she would tell them to me?'

Elsie's eyes and mouth opened. 'I don't know, Master. I should have to ask her.'

'Will you ask her, from me?'

'Ar, Master, I will – and Master?'

'Yes, Elsie?'

'Would you have a word with cook, please, Master?'

'What? Oh, certainly. Don't you worry; don't worry at all.'

But Mr Grimsby forgot, because he was too absorbed in writing down the story of the shilling; and Elsie had to finish all her work before she went to bed. Cold and tired, with aching back and heavy head, she was still scrubbing at greasy pots in cold water at one that morning, and she had to get up again at four. And when she'd lit all the fires and went down to the kitchen, she got a telling off from the cook because the pots and pans weren't as clean as they should be.

Even so, when she went home to see her family, on the one Sunday she had free a month, she still remembered to ask her grandmother if she would tell her stories to Mr Grimsby. Some would say the girl was a fool.

# *Two*

# Mrs Naylor's Story

'It's a chilly day for the Spring, Mrs Naylor.'

'It is an' all, Mr Grimsby — but a drop of this keeps the cold out.'

Mr Grimsby, having filled his guest's glass, filled his own, and then drew towards himself the pile of paper. An ink-stand stood ready, reflected in the polish of the table, and a pen lay beside it.

Mrs Naylor was sipping from her glass and looking up at the shelves of books. 'You'm going to make all these stories of mine into another one of them, am yer?' she asked, nodding her head towards the shelves.

Mr Grimsby smiled again. He had been surprised at how few visits it had taken before the old woman had become quite at home in his house. She no longer bothered to put on her best black Sunday clothes before coming, but simply threw a faded old shawl over her ordinary, limp skirt and blouse. 'It would be pleasant if I could,' he said. 'If I could interest a publisher. I think my little collection worthy of a wider audience.'

11

The old woman was still looking at the books. 'What use am they, though?' she said.

Mr Grimsby found himself at a loss to answer and, after a moment, asked, 'What story is it going to be today?'

'Ooh. I dunno. I told you the one about Half-Dead Ayli, didn't I?'

'You did. A good story.'

'Ooh, I can't think.'

Mr Grimsby shuffled his paper. 'Have you a favourite story, Mrs Naylor?'

'A favourite?'

'Yes. One you like better than all the others.'

'I know what "favourite" means, thank you. I was thinking.' She took another sip of the sherry and, after staring at the floor and thinking, another sip. 'Ar; I've got a favourite. I'll tell you me favourite.'

Mr Grimsby leaned forward to listen.

'There was a witch lived round here once. Ugly he was, ugly big man, but he was wonderful with his hands. He could make anything, make it beautiful – as beautiful as he was ugly hisself. And maybe it wasn't only his hands that was clever! Because his son was beautiful as well – oh, a lovely looking lad. Golden. You could walk for five counties round and never find a better looking lad. Jack his name was. But if he'd missed his Dad's ugliness, he'd missed his cleverness an' all. Stupid, Jack was. Thick as pig—Oh, I beg your pardon, Mr Grimsby. But he wasn't bright at all. An half-baked loaf.

12

'Well, Jack come to his Dad one day, and he says, "Dad, you're so clever, can't you make me some brains? 'Cos, think on, what am I going to do when you'm dead and gone, and I have to make me own way in the world?"

'Now the witch had been thinking that a lot hisself – because you worry about 'em, don't you, Mr Grimsby? – and he said, "I can't make you any brains, Jack, but I can get you some, if you'll do just what I tell you."

' "Tell me," says Jack. "I want some brains."

' "Go into town," says the witch, "and ask about, and bring me back the answer to this question: What runs without any feet?"

'Well, it took a while for Jack to learn the question – I told you he wasn't very bright. Nice lad, but slow, slow. Off he went to town, and he kept stopping people and asking 'em, "What runs without any feet?" Some of 'em just looked at him and went by without saying anything. Some thought he was being funny and pushed him out the road, or told him to sling his hook. Some stopped and had a think, but they couldn't come up with an answer.

'Anyroad, after he'd been going up and down for a while, he come to the market, and he sees a woman at one of the stalls looking at him. Well, women did look at him, they did look! But he didn't think of that; he only thought he'd go and ask her his question. So he did, and her took her time thinking about it, and give him a bit of one of the cheeses her was selling while her was on. Well, the longer her took thinking about it, the longer Jack stayed at her stall. "I'll get it in a minute," her kept saying. "Just let me serve this woman . . ." Her was a nice-looking woman, this market-woman. A bit older than Jack, but not so old. And in the end, when her'd kept him all afternoon, and it was time for her to pack up, her said, "A river. That's what runs without any feet, my lover. A river."

'So Jack went home and told his Dad, and the witch says, "That's right. Who told you?"

' "A woman on the market," Jack says.

' "Would you know her again?" says his Dad. " 'Cos I've got another question. What's yellow and shining, but aint gold? If I was you, I'd go and ask that same woman."

'So Jack spent all night learning the question and, the next day, he's off to town again. And he goes straight to the market, and the woman, and he asks her, "What's yellow and shining, but aint gold?"

' "Oh, I can't think just now," says the woman. "Hang on while I serve these people." And then he had to hang on while her tidied her stall up; and then her asked him to share a bit of dinner with her, and then there was more people to serve – and one way and another, her kept him with her all day again. Well, I wouldn't blame her. There wasn't a better looking lad in the whole town. But right at the end of the day, when the market was packing up, her said, "The answer's 'the sun'. Or gorse-blossom, if you like. Or yellow apples on a shady tree. But I'd say, 'the sun' myself."

'Round Jack turned and home he went, and he told the

answers to his Dad. "That's right," says the witch. "You're closer to your brains than you was." And the next morning he gives Jack a fleecy skin off a sheep and he says, "I want you to take this to market and sell it, and bring me back the skin and the money you sold it for."

'Well, I told you Jack was daft. He was too daft to see how hard that'd be. So off he went to town, and straight to his friend on the market. But her says that her only sells fruit and veg, and cheese sometimes, so her can't help him. Off he goes round all the other market stalls. Some folk was happy to buy the fleece, but when they found out that he wanted to take it home with him, as well as the money, they said, "Get off out of it, you sawnie! Clear off, you malkin!" they said. "You can have the money or the fleece, but not both," they told him. "Coming here, trying to make we as big fools as you!" they said. "Sling your hook afore I ding your ear-hole!"

'Poor lad, he was in a right state – because his Dad had told him to bring back the fleece and the money, you see, and he always did what his Dad said, because he hadn't got the brains to think for hisself. And the market-woman sees him, and her sees he's all upset, so her calls him over and asks him what's the matter. Well, he tells her, and her laughs and says, "That's no problem! Sell me the fleece!"

'So he sold her the fleece, and her give him a good price for it. And then, while he watches, her gets a sharp knife and shears all the wool off it. Then her gives Jack the skin back, and tells him to wrap his money up in it, so he won't lose it on the way home. And then her goes and sells the wool to another stall. And with the money her buys herself a pint, and Jack half-a-pint, and her sends him home.

' "That's a clever woman," says the old witch, when Jack gets back with the skin and the money. "And her cares for you, don't her? What's her name?"

' "I think folk call her Gill," says Jack.

' "One more question," says the old witch, "and then I think you'll have your brains."

' "Oh, tell me the question," says Jack. "I want them brains."

' "This is it: What animal is it that goes on four legs, then two legs, then three legs?"

'Into town Jack goes the next day, straight to Gill's stall, and he asks her this question. "Oh, I shall have to think hard about that," her says, and her keeps him with her all day, and gets him to help her on the stall. And he's not so bad, if you tell him what to do, and when it comes to shifting heavy boxes about, he's strong and willing. And when he's just standing behind the stall, he's a decoration. And at the end of the day, her says, "The answer to your question – the animal's a man. He crawls on all fours as a babby, walks on two legs when he's growed, and leans on a stick like a three-legged thing when he's old. Off you go now, and go safe." And her gives him a kiss and an apple to take with him.

'Jack takes this answer back to his Dad, and the next day it's the witch himself who goes into town. He finds the fruit and veg stall and says to the woman behind it, "Bin you Gill?"

' "I be," her says, "and I'd bet my last shilling you'm Jack's Dad."

' "I be," says the witch, "and seeing as it's dinner-time, will you come and have a sup and a bite with me?" And he offers her his arm. So her goes with him to a tavern, and they have a pint and a pie, and they talk and laugh, and like each other a lot. And at the end, the witch says, "My son needs brains. Will you marry him, Gill, and be his brains?"

' "I will," says Gill. "I'm a clever woman, and the best husband for a clever woman is a pretty fool — and that's your Jack!"

'And when they told Jack that he was marrying Gill, he was as happy as a pig in — Oh, excuse me, Master. He was happy. He hadn't had the brains to see what his old Dad was driving at, sending him to ask all them questions, but he liked Gill, and he liked the kiss Gill had given him, and since he'd spent all his life doing what his Dad told him, he didn't mind spending the rest of it doing what Gill told him.

'So they got married, and Gill went to live with Jack and his Dad. It was wonderful the way they all got on. You could tell Gill was Jack's brains, because he was never far away from her. And the better the old witch got to know his daughter-in-law, the better he liked her, and he taught her a lot of what he knowed, and her picked up a lot more

17

from watching him. "I thought I hadn't got a child who'd keep my skills alive," he said, "but now I have."

' "And will have more," Gill said. "And they'll all be as pretty as Jack and as clever as me."

'But then, what happened was, the King come to see the witch. The King wanted a palace built for him, the biggest, richest and most beautifullest palace in the world, a palace like no other king in the world had. "Can you build me a palace like that?" the King said.

' "With me son to help me, I could," said the witch. And he promised to come and build a palace for the King. Afore they set off, Gill kissed Jack and said, "Make sure you'm good friends with all the King's servants. Speak well to 'em, and always say, 'hello' and 'goodbye' as you go in and out. It's always a good thing to have friends in a King's court, so I've heard."

' "That's good advice from your wife, as usual, Jack," says the witch, and him and Jack kissed Gill goodbye, and off they went.

'Building the palace didn't take so long, not with the witch on the job. He'd start with the roof, and put the walls under it after, and then knock holes in 'em for the doors and windows. Then he'd run up a tower and lay a few floors. Everything was beautiful and ornamented, with coloured glass and paintings and gold – it was the finest workmanship ever seen. Every day the King come to see how things were getting on; and every day the witch and Jack went out of their way to be pleasant and friendly to all

18

the King's servants and companions, just like Gill had told them.

'In a week the palace seemed finished, and the King went all through it, and he couldn't have been more pleased. "Perfect!" he said. "Not another king in the world has a palace like this! Just wait till they see it!"

' "There is one more thing," said the witch. "There's this little room – I don't suppose you noticed, King, it's only a little place – but the ceiling isn't finished. It'll be done tomorrow."

' "Then I'll come back tomorrow and pay you for the building," said the King; and he got on his horse and rode off. But one of his servants hung back and said to the witch, "A quiet word to you. The King wants to make sure that no other palace anything like this is ever built anywhere in the world, so beware." Then he rode after the King.

'Jack says to his Dad, "What did he mean, Dad?"

' "He meant," says the witch, "that the King is going to kill us tomorrow, so we can't ever build a palace for another king. So you see how good Gill's advice was, to make friends with the servants!"

'Well, Jack was daft, but he knowed what being killed meant. "I shan't ever see Gill again!" he said. "Dad! What am we going to do?"

' "Don't fret, don't fret," his Dad said. "Leave it to your brains." And he got on and finished the last of the work on the palace.

'Next day, when the King come, the witch says to him, "Sorry, but the palace still isn't finished. See, there's a special tool I need, and I forgot to bring it with me. But if you pay us for our work, to save you coming again, Jack and me will just nip home to get the tool, and come back and finish up."

' "Oh no," says the King. "I can't allow you to go. You might not come back and then my palace would never be finished."

' "Then let me son go," says the witch. 'He can fetch the tool for me."

' "Oh no," says the King. "Your son stays here with you."

' "Then send a messenger to my son's wife, to ask for the tool," says the witch.

' "That I'll do," says the King.

' "The messenger must say this to her," says the witch. "He must say, 'Give me Crooked and Straight'!"

'And off went a messenger to the witch's house, and he hammered on the door. Gill was up the stairs, and her stuck her head out of a window. "What do you want?" her says.

' "In the name of the King," he says, "give me Crooked and Straight! Quick! It's needed!"

' "Crooked and Straight?" says Gill. "I don't know what you mean."

' "It's for the witch," says the messenger. "It's a tool he needs to finish the palace. Hand it over, now, on the King's orders!"

' "Oh," Gill says, and her thinks very quick. "Oh, I can't," her says. "That's a very special, rare, expensive tool, that is. I dare not give it to anybody except my husband or his father. How do I know you won't steal it?"

' "I'm a royal messenger! I'm trusted with royal letters and jewels, so I'm sure I can be trusted with a workman's tool!"

' "Oh no," says Gill. "A tool's worth much more to a workman than jewels am to a King. And that tool's the most precious thing we have, and I won't give it to anybody but my husband or his father – except, maybe, the King hisself, or his son."

' And nothing the messenger said could make her change her mind. So the messenger had to gallop back to the King and tell him. "The woman's very stupid," he said. "She won't give the tool to anybody except Jack or his Dad."

' "Nobody else?" the King asked.

' "Well . . . Yourself, Your Majesty, or your son," says the messenger.

' "Son!" says the King. "Come here! I'm sending you to fetch a tool."

'So the King's son, all dressed up in gold and jewels, with a gold crown on his head, rode over to the witch's house and shouted, "Come out, woman, and give me Crooked and Straight!"

'Gill come to the door and her says, "Oh, you'll have to come in, Your Highness, because the tool's kept in a big chest, and I can't lift the lid. It's too heavy for me."

'The prince sighed and grumbled at all the trouble he was being put to, but his Dad would ding his head if he went back without the tool, so he gets down off his hoss and goes into the house. Gill showed him an enormous chest, and he wasn't surprised her couldn't lift the lid. "I'll soon have that open," he said. And so he did, but as soon as he had the lid lifted, Gill come behind him, grabbed him by the legs, and bundled him into the big chest, crown, spurs, gold cloak and all. Down with the lid, a turning of the key, and there's the prince, a prisoner, and all bent-up and crooked, and he couldn't get out no-how.

' "There!" says Gill. "You'm Crooked and Strait! Just like Dad said."

'Then Gill sat at the table and wrote a letter to the King – because her was a clever woman and writing a letter was nothing to her. It told the King what her'd done with the Prince, and it said that her wouldn't let him out of the chest until Jack and his Dad come home safe, with their wages paid in full, and a faithful promise that the King wouldn't try to hurt them no more.

'When the King got the letter, he knowed he was out-done, and he sent for the witch and paid him everything he owed him. And he made him a solemn promise, in front of witnesses, that he'd never try to hurt him or Jack again. And then he let them go.

'Home Jack and his Dad went, as fast as they could and, as soon as they got there, Jack hugged Gill, and Gill hugged

Jack, and the witch let the prince out of the chest and sent him packing, with his spurs bent and his crown slipping off his head.

' "Daughter," says the witch to Gill, "I shall make you a palace bigger and richer and more beautiful than the one I built for the King." And so he did, and the three of 'em lived in it as happy as the birds in the trees; and happier still when Gill and Jack had a daughter and a son who was as handsome as their father and as clever as their mother.

'And I was at the christening, and got more than a little tiddly, Mr Grimsby, if you'll believe me – but then I come away – and I come away saying that the best husband for a clever woman is a pretty fool.' And Mrs Naylor rocked back in her chair and laughed.

'If only there were such a clever woman for every fool,' said Mr Grimsby.

'Oh, they baint so far and few between,' said Mrs Naylor. 'You look round, Mr Grimsby. You'll see more than one good-looking, strutting fool married to a clever woman.' She held her glass in place and smiled as Mr Grimsby filled it again. 'Oh!' she said, with a sudden squeak. 'I know what I've got to tell you – I had a word with Sergeant Lamb, like you asked, and he said he'd be happy to tell you his stories, but he can't come here. You'll have to go to him.'

'Oh, but Mrs Naylor, you know I don't get about as I used.'

'You get about better than Sergeant Lamb – he's only got the one leg.'

'Oh dear.'

'He was a soldier. He was in that battle – oh, d'you know, it's gone right out of my head now. Funny name. It was a famous victory, I do know. He was in it, y'know, the Duke with the big nose.'

'Good Lord!' said Mr Grimsby. 'You don't mean Waterloo?'

'That's it! Waterloo! I knowed it was a funny name. He was at Waterloo, was our Sergeant Lamb, and he left his leg there. So you'll have to go to him.'

'Well! A hero of Waterloo!' Mr Grimsby said. 'I think perhaps I could make an effort for such an illustrious gentleman.'

'And – I hope you don't mind me saying this, Mr Grimsby—?'

'Oh, we're good friends, Mrs Naylor. What is it?'

'Well – you know it's a treat for me to come here and sit by your fire, and you're so good as to fill me glass and feed me a little bit of cake, and I do enjoy coming here and telling you me stories – but the Sergeant, he's a bit of an harder case than I am, if you see what I mean.'

'Ah – you mean that Sergeant Lamb requires—?'

'Summat in the way of payment, if you don't mind, Mr Grimsby.'

'Well . . .' Mr Grimsby sat back in his chair and clasped his hands together over his belly. 'Did Sergeant Lamb, by

24

any chance, hint to you how much—?'

'Oh, not money, Mr Grimsby, not money, no. But Sergeant Lamb, he likes a bit of a drink now and then – and his wooden leg's always going through his trousers. At the knee, y'know – so if you've got some old pairs—?'

'I see. Well, of course, of course . . . And, er, perhaps yourself, Mrs Naylor, for the many stories you've told me? Is there, perhaps—?'

Mrs Naylor set her glass on the table with a sharp click. She pulled her shawl from the back of her chair and wrapped it about herself. 'I wasn't asking for myself, Mr Grimsby, but for Sergeant Lamb, who's a good friend of mine. I shall have to be going now.'

'Oh Mrs Naylor—' Mr Grimsby rose. 'I haven't offended you, I hope? I meant no offence.'

'I shall have to be on my way. Goodbye, Mr Grimsby. If I don't see you again, I hope you keep in good health.'

Mr Grimsby hurried to open the door for her. 'I do hope I shall see you again, Mrs Naylor.'

But Mrs Naylor was clattering away down his hall towards the kitchen door, where she would find her granddaughter, and she didn't look back.

# Three

# Sergeant Lamb's Story

The black pig lay on its side in the little sty and snored. Mr Grimsby and Sergeant Lamb sat on the sty's brick wall, and the Sergeant poured rum into the glass Mr Grimsby held, from the bottle which Mr Grimsby had brought for him. The Sergeant's hand shook slightly, as it always did, but he was careful with rum, and it all went into the glass.

'That's the stuff to give the troops,' Sergeant Lamb said.

Mr Grimsby held the rum to his nose and sniffed deeply at the strong vapours. Quite near him was the swill-pail, balanced on its hearth of fire-blackened bricks, and the stench from it was appalling, a sickly, strong stink of garbage and staleness, boiled together. The caked trough in the sty stank too, and it was altogether a most noisome spot. Mr Grimsby would never have chosen to sit there himself, but Sergeant Lamb sat for hours on the wall of his pigsty, gazing out over the rough, yellow fields to the walls of the factories. He didn't seem to notice the smell and Mr Grimsby was too polite to mention it.

When Sergeant Lamb had filled his own glass, Mr

27

Grimsby raised his and said, 'To the victors of Waterloo!'

'Hum,' said Sergeant Lamb and rested his glass of rum on his left leg, which ended at mid-thigh. His crutch leaned against the wall behind him. He rarely wore his wooden leg, because it hurt him.

Mr Grimsby, embarrassed, looked back at the little house, one of a row of five cottages. Their bricks had been grimed to a dark and sullen red, and the lower parts of the wall were green with moss. The door was as low and narrow as a coffin.

From the door, a straight path of black and grey cinders led to the sty, and on either side of the path were beds of brown earth planted with dull green vegetables. It was a drab sight – nor was the view over the fields any prettier. Long yellow grass and nettles grew there round stubby black thorn trees with few leaves. A shaggy brown and white horse grazed at the end of its tether, and behind it there were more grimed, dark-red walls. The clash and crash of drop-hammers, and the clamour of beaten metal carried across the field to them. If it hadn't been for the reek of the pig-swill, they would have smelt the hot coals, the hot metal, the burnt and burning smells of the foundries that clanged and rang all round them.

Sergeant Lamb sipped his rum and, into the stink and the clamour, said:

'It was at Waterloo that Wellington comes galloping up to me, and "Joe!" he says, "Joe!"

' "What is it, Arthur?" I says.

'He says, "Do you see them Frenchies up on top of that ridge there?"

' "I see 'em," I says.

' "Take some men and see 'em off," he says. "Take plenty. Take – oh – twenty-four."

' "Rightio, Art," I says, and I went to find me corporal. "See them Frenchies up on the ridge, Corp," I says. "How many do you reckon there be?"

'He takes a squint. "Oh – four hundred," he says.

' "And how many men do you think we'll need to run 'em off?" I says.

' "Oh – about ten."

' "That's what I figured," I says, "but Wellington, he says to take twenty-four. Tell you what," I says, "to keep the old man happy, we'll take fifteen."

' "More than enough," says the Corp.

'So we picked our fifteen men, and off we went. We was just getting to the ridge when round the corner on it comes Napoleon, on his white 'oss with his hat on wrong. He says, "Joe, Joe, where you going?"

'I says, "Just to the top of the ridge to see off them beggars up there."

'And he says, "Oh no!" And he gallops his 'oss up in front on we, shouting, "Joe and fifteen of his lads am coming! Run! Run!" And they all run like hares. So we cleared the ridge and took the easy road back.

'And I went to report to Wellington. "We cleared the ridge, Arthur," I says.

' "I know, I know," he says – he'd been watching through his spy-glass. "What I want to know, Joe," he says, "is who was that bloke on the white 'oss you was talking to?" '

Mr Grimsby laughed quietly, and Sergeant Lamb smiled, raised his trembling hand and poured more rum into their glasses. They went on sitting on the pigsty wall. A scream from a steam-valve sounded from one of the factories, and made the brown and white horse lift its head.

'I know another one,' said Sergeant Lamb, 'about a lad that took the Queen's shilling, and become a soldier; and he was in a battle, with the guns cracking the sky open, and the balls flying through the smoke, and the musket-shot rattling, and hosses screaming, and shells banging and the men yelling – and then he was in this country lane, and it was all quiet. And he walked along this lane and at the end of it's the Pearly Gates. "I must be dead," he thinks, "and I've come to Heaven. I'm in luck!" Because he never thought he'd get to Heaven.

'So he goes up to the Gates, and he knocks, and an Angel answers. "Who'm you?" the Angel says.

'He salutes and gives his name, rank and number. "We'm not expecting you," says the Angel. "No; no—" He starts looking through papers, the Angel does. "No, I've got nothing about you down here. Stay here, while I go and check."

'And the Angel goes off and leaves the soldier standing by the Gate.

'Well, the soldier waits a bit. Then he thinks he might as well have a look inside Heaven while he's waiting – where's the harm? So he edges in through the Gate. And it's all very fine in there. All made of clouds and stars, very beautiful. But the Angel don't come back, and the soldier thinks he'll have a bit of an explore. He can't hurt owt, just having a reccy. So he wanders off.

'He has a look here – and he has a look there – he sees more wonderful things than I've got time to tell on – and then he comes to a flight of steps. Up he climbs, and up and up, higher and higher – and, at the top of the steps, he sees a chair. It's God's Chair, where God sits and looks out over the whole world, and sees everything we do.

'Our lad thinks it must be a wonderful view from that chair – and it can't hurt to have a look, can it? So he stands on tip-toe and reaches up to the edge of the chair with his hands, and he uses his feet to scramble up, and he clambers on to the seat. It's so big that he can stand up and walk about on it – it'd make a good big gun-platform. And, standing up there, he looked out – and he saw all the world. All the world and all that was going on. He saw what God sees.

'There's happiness in this world, but there's more un-happiness . . . If the happiness is raindrops, then the unhappiness is oceans, deep, deep cold oceans. The soldier looked out over the world, and he saw thousands dying of hunger, and thousands more grieving over them that died – and every death was as sharp to him as it was to them that suffered it, every death was as sharp as bayonets . . . He saw thousands of mothers grieving over sick childer, or dead childer; he saw thousands of fathers weeping.

'There was childer crying for dead mothers and dead fathers; there was husbands crying for dead wives, and wives crying for dead husbands . . .

'There's no loss like death. When you lose somebody, there's no finding 'em again, however you hunt. There's no seeing 'em again, ever. No hearing 'em again, ever. It don't matter how many promises they made to always be with you, never to leave you – every man, every woman, every child, is shovelled into the earth, sooner or later; and the more you loved 'em, the more you grieve . . . The more you grieve . . .

'And we kill each other. The soldier saw battlefields, in every part of the world, battlefields – and the wounded lying, hurting, dying, scared . . . Calling out for help, and no help coming . . .

'He saw the rich getting richer by making the poor poorer, cheating 'em and underpaying 'em, selling 'em bad food and charging high rents, and sending 'em out to fight their battles and die for 'em, while they got rich by selling the guns that blowed folk apart – and then laughing about it, and calling the poor folk stupid and dirty . . .

'He saw the poor folk having hard time of it, going cold, going hungry, going tired and worried and sad day after day . . . Saw the poor women giving their food to the childer and husband and going without theirselves, going in rags . . . Saw the childer with no toys to play with being sent out to work, being chained to machines and beaten to make 'em work, to fill the pockets of the rich . . .

'He saw the sick, in mortal pain, and there nothing that could help 'em . . . He saw robbers robbing folk as poor as themselves, and leaving them hurt and bleeding and scared and penniless . . . He saw the lonely, sore at heart, day after day, and nobody caring, nobody giving 'em a word . . . And some of the sick, the robbed, the lonely, were rich, but it didn't make 'em any kinder to the poor . . .

'He saw bullies, hurting people with fists and kicks and words, day after day hurting people, and enjoying it and laughing about it, and nobody helping the people they bullied . . .

'He saw the people disappointed when promises was broke and trust was broke and lies was told. He saw the childer beaten, the women beaten, the men flogged . . .

'He saw the ones who try hard, try hard all their lives and never, never win . . . He saw that the whole world, the whole world, was one great ache of pain and misery. And he lay down on the seat of God's chair, and he wept, he cried as if his heart would swell and crack his ribs. If you saw what he saw, you'd do the same. He saw what God sees: the truth. He saw the world for what it is.

'And the Angel come and found him, and knowed what was up. "Now, now," says the Angel, and picks him up and sits him on its lap. "You weren't supposed to come up here, you weren't supposed to see this. You aren't made of strong enough stuff, you men. Listen," says the Angel, patting his back, "stop your crying now, and I'll read to you from God's book. Come on now, dry your eyes and stop making that noise in Heaven."

'And the Angel read from God's book, that He keeps by His chair, to read when looking at the world gets too much even for Him. The book was about what the world would be like if men and women was kind to each other – only that. If they was just kind to each other.

'There'd be no wars, because if people was kind to each other, there'd be no wars to fight. So no men would lie crying on battlefields, and no widows, no orphans would be made by the guns.

'There'd be no poor, because if people was kind to each other and helped each other, them with a million pounds would give most of it away to them that hadn't got anything. Then nobody would starve because they hadn't got even one penny. No childer would go without food, or medicine, or learning . . .

'And the soldier stopped crying, and he sat up straight on the Angel's lap, and listened . . .

'People wouldn't steal from each other, or attack each other, said the Angel: no childer would be beaten, nobody would be lonely. The sick and the old would always have somebody to care for them, and nobody would be afraid because they'd always know that their neighbour would help them . . . "All people have to do is to be kind, and to love each other," said the Angel. "It would be so easy to

34

turn the sad world into the world in this book."

' "It would!" said the soldier. "It would!" Because, right then, he thought that it would. It seemed like the easiest thing there could be – easier than squeezing a trigger.

' "But you've got to go back to Earth now," says the Angel. "You come here by mistake and we're not ready for you yet." And the Angel lifts him down from God's chair, takes his hand and leads him back to the Gate. When they got there, the Angel took out its handkerchief, and spit on it, and wiped his face and had him blow his nose, and then the Angel kissed him and pushed him out of Heaven. "Ta-ra," says the Angel. "See you in a bit."

'And the soldier's back in the lane, and he follows it back to Earth.

'He wakes up in a field hospital, with his leg off, and straightaway he starts telling the blokes on either side of him what the Angel had read to him from the book. "We've only got to be kind to each other!" he says, and the one laughs at him. The other was dying.

' "We've only got to be kind to each other!" he shouts out to whoever'd listen, and they said he was sick, and raving, and that he'd die soon hisself.

'But he didn't. He got out of the hospital, and he got shipped back to England, with a wooden leg and a crutch, and everybody he met, he told about the Angel and the book. "We've only got to be kind to each other – if we'd only be kind to each other—"

' "You'm mad, you'm barmy," they all said.

'He tried being kind. He tried to share his food, and had it all taken from him. He went to help a man fallen in a gutter, and the man was a robber, and beat him with a club, and stole the last of his money and his jacket. He tried to help a woman who was being thumped by a man, and got his face scratched and his eye blacked. "You'm mad, you'm barmy," that's all anybody would say to him.

'What he'd seen from God's chair was true. The world was full of pain and misery – there was a great big, granite mountain of pain and misery, and all the kindness was like little raindrops trying to wash it away.

'And the soldier started to forget what the Angel had said. He could only remember the aching and the misery he'd felt when he'd looked out over the world. And the only cure for that ache was God's own book, by God's chair, and the words in it, and to hear them words read by an Angel. But there was no finding that lane that led up to the Pearly Gates.

'But anyroad, our soldier died in the end, and maybe he's up there now, listening to the Angel . . . Or maybe he missed the road, and he's down in the other place, stewing in a pot. It can't be much worse than here. I reckon that's what Hell is, Mr Grimsby – it's this world of ours, seen clear, seen for what it is. That's why I keep drinking this stuff . . .' And the Sergeant raised his glass of rum in his constantly trembling hand. 'The last thing I want is to see clear.'

Mr Grimsby was silent. Flakes of soot from a factory

chimney, light and fluttering as black snowflakes, fell around them as they sat on the pigsty wall. The clamour and crash and drang of beaten metal sounded across the rough fields, but the shaggy horse grazed undisturbed, quite used to the din.

Mr Grimsby cleared his throat. 'A fine story, Sergeant.'

The Sergeant smiled his slow, stiff smile, and picked up the bottle of rum from the pigsty wall. He was a silent man, except when telling stories. As he poured rum into the bottom of the glasses, a cart went by on the road, with a clatter of hooves, a rattle and crash of wheels, a creaking of wooden joints and leather harness, adding to the din from the factories.

Mr Grimsby took his glass and raised it. 'Let's drink to our hopes of Heaven!'

The Sergeant raised his own glass. 'And here's to meeting me leg again!'

*Four*

# Mrs Riley's Story

'Mr Grimsby, sir,' said Elsie, 'there's a man wants to see you.'

'Oh?'

'At the kitchen door, sir.'

'Did he say why he wanted to see me?'

'Oh . . . It's about these stories, sir, that you keep listening to. Something about these stories, anyroad.'

'Ah!' said Mr Grimsby. His interest was caught at once. 'I shall be down, Elsie, presently.'

In the bright sunlight of the little yard, when Mr Grimsby looked out of the cool kitchen, stood a man, his back to the door. His dark clothes hung on him, making him a dark splodge on the bright, white paving of the yard. 'You wished to see me?' Mr Grimsby said.

The man started and turned quickly. He tossed his head to throw his long, fair forelock out of his eyes and looked at Mr Grimsby, for an instant, with frightened eyes before giving a big, nervous gulp and looking away. He muttered something.

Mr Grimsby, amused, leaned from the door. 'What?'

The young man gave him a direct stare and almost shouted, 'Are you him that wants stories? – Sir.'

'I do collect stories, for my sins, yes. Why? Have you a story for me?'

'Not me, sir, no sir. Me mother, sir. Could you – could you come now, sir?' And the young man half-turned from the door, as if ready to go.

'Now? What – at once?' Mr Grimsby smiled. 'Is there so much hurry?'

'Yessir.' The young man turned his head away. 'Me mother's dying, sir.'

'Oh.' Mr Grimsby withdrew a little, back into his shady kitchen. The young man, in his dark, shabby clothes, remained framed in the brightness of the yard.

The young man faced Mr Grimsby again, and the sunlight gleamed on the stubble on his chin. 'I can pay for your time, sir.'

'Pay! Good gracious—! My boy, there's no call to talk of payment!'

'But will you come, sir? Me mother, her wants to tell her stories, sir – to somebody who'll remember 'em. I can't remember 'em. I haven't the knack of it.'

'Wait,' Mr Grimsby said. 'Wait while I get my hat – and my notebook – I'll be a moment.'

Mrs Riley lay in bed in a small, square downstairs room, which the bed almost filled. A fire burned in the big black range alongside the bed, and made the little room so hot that the door had to be left open, and the breeze ruffled the sheets of newsprint that curtained the window.

'Thank you for coming, sir,' said the sick woman, and Mr Grimsby, seated on a hard chair beside the bed, murmured that it was his pleasure and she was to think nothing of it. 'All me life I've loved the stories,' she said. 'And I can't bear to think of taking 'em with me when I go, and them never being told again . . . It's no use telling him, good lad though he is . . . He's got too much to think on, can't keep 'em in his head – can't tell 'em anyroad . . . You'll write 'em down, so anybody can learn 'em? You will write 'em down, won't you?'

'I will write them down, I promise you, Mrs Riley.'

'What shall I tell? What one shall I tell. Here . . . my lad loved to hear this one when he was little . . .

'Once upon a time – not in your time, nor in my time, or in anybody else's time, but in a good time – there lived this old pair who had three daughters. All three was pretty things, but the eldest, well, her was just the apple of her Daddy's eye, her Mother's first-born. I don't suppose they meant to make more of her than her sisters, but they couldn't help it, and the sisters, they was jealous.

'Anyroad – listen – the old man's going to town one day, and he says to his three wenches, 'What shall I bring you back, me lovers?' he says.

41

'And the youngest, her says, "Oh, bring me back a bunch of blue ribbons—"

'And the next, her says, "Oh bring me back sixpenn'orth of best lace."

'But the eldest, her says, "Bring me back what you know I'd like."

'So – listen – off the old man goes to town, and when he's ready to come home again, he goes to the market to buy the presents. Well, the ribbons and the lace am easy found, easy bought, but he walks round and round the stalls looking for what his eldest would like. He almost gives up, but he thinks, "I can't go home with a present for the other two and none for me first-born."

'And he come across this stall where an old woman was selling all manner of junk. And there was this pretty little saucer, a little white saucer all gilded pretty, the kind you can see your fingers through. And sitting in the saucer was a rosy apple. Soon as he saw it, he knew that was what his eldest girl would like, so he bought it, soon as he saw it, and took it home.

'He give the ribbons to his youngest – "Oh, blue ribbons, thank you, Daddy!" And he give the lace to his second – "Oh, pretty lace, thank you, Daddy!" And then he give his eldest the little white, goldy saucer and the rosy apple, and her give him a kiss on the cheek.

' "An old saucer and an apple," said her sisters. "What you want them for?" But her didn't say nothing, her just went into the garden and sat on the step, where the big bushes of blue lavender grow. Her put the rosy apple in the saucer and her spun it round.

'Round and round it spun, red and green and white and gold, and while it spun it made pictures in the air – visions – all kinds of pictures – and her sisters come and stood over her to watch. And her Mom and Dad come, and they stared.

'Pictures of the sea they saw – the water going up, tall as houses, and going on and on to the sky. Ships they saw, with their masts and sails, and they'd never seen ships before. Soldiers, marching, marching, and rivers and towns and cathedrals, and ladies wearing frocks that'd buy a kingdom. They saw into all the strange lands there am, and all the strange people – until the apple stopped spinning in the saucer, and then it all went away.

' "Spin it again!" said the sisters, but the eldest, her wouldn't. Her didn't want to get tired of it.

' "Let we have it!" said the sisters, but the eldest, her wouldn't. Her knowed they'd break it.

'So her sisters hated her even more, because they wanted the saucer and the apple. They thought: if her was dead, we'd get the blessed saucer, and people wouldn't be going round saying how wonderful her was all the time. So they planned how they'd get rid of her, and they said to her, "Let's go picking mushrooms tomorrow." And the next day they all got up early and went out into the fields while it was still dark and the grass was still wet, picking the little white mushrooms . . . And they come to the river. And the two sisters, they pushed the eldest in. They pushed her in, and they stood on the bank and they watched her drown. The water carried her away in her white frock, floating like a swan. And when they'd seen the last of her, they went back home and had their breakfast. That's how some folk am. They ate the breakfast, and when their Mom and Dad said, "Where's your sister?" they said, "How should we know?"

'But the little goldy saucer and the rosy apple was theirs now. As soon as they'd had their breakfast, they fetched it, and spun it, and thought they'd see all sorts of wonders – but all the apple showed them was their sister floating down the river, so they hid it, and they didn't want to spin it no more.

'The old man and woman was waiting for their daughter to come home, but her didn't come and her didn't come. "Let's wait a bit longer," they said, because they didn't want to think anything had happened. Still her didn't come. It was getting dark and there wasn't sight nor sound of her. "Let's spin the apple in the saucer," they said. "Maybe it'll show we where her is." But they couldn't find it. All the next day the old man was out looking, and the old woman kept going to the door and looking up and down for a sight of her first-born, but her didn't come back to them. And the two sisters, when they saw how much their Mom and Dad thought of the eldest, they was glad they'd drowned her and got rid of her.

'But listen! The river took the oldest sister and carried

44

her miles away; miles and miles away. It washed her up in the shade of some big trees, and there her lay, with the water washing round her, and the leaves falling down on her, and her hair spread out round her.

'And this young lad comes by – he's on the road, looking for work, and he's playing his fiddle as he goes along, to get money for food. And as he's going by the river, he sees something white through the trees, so down the bank he climbs, and he finds her lying there in her white frock. He leans over her a long time, just looking, her's so beautiful. He can't take his eyes away. He thinks, if he does, he'll forget just how her looks, and he wants to remember.

'But he knows he can't look at her forever, and that he should away and tell somebody about her, and get her buried. But he wants a keepsake, so he takes out his knife, and cuts off some of her long yellow hair, and puts it in his pocket. And then he ups and gets him to the nearest houses, and tells 'em about the beautiful girl who's lying drowned under the trees by the riverside. And out they all go and carry her back to the church. And everybody's standing round looking at her because her's so lovely. Then they start saying, "How come he was the one who knowed where her was?"

' "Because he was the one who pushed her in!"

' "Because he killed her!"

' "He's a murderer!"

'Well, he says he never did anybody any harm, but they don't believe him, and they take him and lock him up, and they'm going to hang him for murdering the girl soon as they get time. But for the minute they'm too busy burying the girl. Everybody in the town comes to the funeral, and people am so sorry for her they put money together and buy her a proper service, and a stone for her grave – but her's buried outside the churchyard, since her's a stranger. Still, an old yew tree leans over the wall and drops red berries into the grass growing over her.

'All this while the young fiddler's been in the lock-up, thinking about what's going to happen to him, and not happy at all. But then he thinks, What the Hell, and he takes the girl's yellow hair out of his pocket and he passes the time making strings out of it, and he strings his fiddle with it. And then he puts bow to fiddle and he starts to play.

'But instead of fiddle-music, there comes a girl's voice – the strings of yellow hair play with a girl's voice, and it sings:

> "*Free the fiddler, set him free,*
> *Hey, the green green garlanding,*
> *He never did any harm to me,*
> *Oh, the bonny, bonny bunch of lavender!*"

'Well, people passing by the lock-up heard this singing coming from inside, and they had the lock-up opened, and they see nobody there but the fiddler, playing on his yellow strings. So they fetch him out, and he plays his fiddle through the streets of the town, with crowds of people following him, and everywhere he goes, the fiddle sings:

> *"Free the fiddler, set him free,*
> *Hey, the green green garlanding,*
> *He never did any harm to me,*
> *Oh, the bonny, bonny bunch of lavender!"*

'So they let him go – and he goes, fast as he can!

'The next town he come to, he went to the market-place and started playing his fiddle – but when he drew his bow across the strings, they started to sing in a woman's voice, a lovely woman's voice:

> *"How my mother's tears will fall,*
> *Hey, the green, green garlanding,*
> *When she hears of my burial*
> *Oh, the bonny, bonny bunch of lavender.*
>
> *How my father he will moan,*
> *Hey, the green, green garlanding,*
> *When he hears that I have gone,*
> *Oh, the bonny, bonny bunch of lavender."*

'And that's all the fiddle would play, bow as he liked. Nothing else would it play. And it was so strange to hear a fiddle singing like a woman, and so beautiful, that everyone come round to hear it. Even the dogs and cats come round, and the birds in the air come down to hear and perched on the fiddler's shoulders and sung round his head. And the people thought it was such a grand sight, they filled the fiddler's hat with money.

'So the fiddler went on, and everywhere he set bow to fiddle, he made lots of money, but the fiddle would only play that one song, and it sounded just like a woman singing. By and by he come – though he didn't know it – he come to the place where the dead girl's Mom and Dad was living. And he stopped in the market-place, like he always did, and he started playing, and all the people come round, and the dogs and cats and birds, and even the mice and rats come to hear. And the dead girl's Mom and Dad and her two sisters happened to be in town that day, and they come an' all. And as soon as they was in the crowd, the fiddle started to sing a different song.

"*There she stands, my mother dear,*
*Hey, the green, green garlanding,*
*There he stands, my father dear,*
*Oh, the bonny, bonny bunch of lavender.*

*There she stands, my sister Anne,*
*Hey, the green, green garlanding,*
*By the river, she pushed me in,*
*Oh, the bonny, bonny bunch of lavender.*

48

> *There she stands, my sister May,*
> *Hey, the green, green garlanding,*
> *How she laughed as I drowned that day,*
> *Oh, the bonny, bonny bunch of lavender."*

'Well, the old man and the old woman, they knowed their daughter's voice, and they cried out, and they wept – and the two sisters, they knowed their sister's voice, and they cried out that they'd never done it—And the old man and the old woman pushed through the crowd and got hold of the fiddler and shook him and said, "Tell us where our daughter is, tell us, tell us!"

'So the fiddler told 'em how he found the beautiful girl drowned in the river, and how her was buried, and how he made his fiddle strings from her hair. And he offers to take 'em to her grave. They thanked him for that, and the old woman, her hunted through the house, harder than her'd ever hunted before, and her found the little saucer and the rosy apple where it had been hidden, and her put it in her apron pocket.

' "It was the last thing her asked we for," her said. "We'll put it with her in her last place."

'So they all set off, the fiddler, and the old man and the old woman, and they drag the two sisters along, and some of the town-people follow along an' all, to see what'll happen.

'Well, they come to the poor little grave, outside the churchyard wall, with the red yew berries lying in the

49

green grass. And the old man and the old woman, they can't stop crying, but the sisters' eyes am dry. And the old man he says, "Play your fiddle, fiddler – let's hear our little girl's voice one more time."

'But the fiddler don't play. He puts his fiddle down on the grave, and the strings quiver, and the fiddle starts playing all by itself – it sings all by itself in the girl's voice.

> "*Plant the apple on my grave,*
> *Hey, the green, green garlanding,*
> *And I will rise and live again,*
> *Oh, the bonny, bonny bunch of lavender.*"

'Well the mother had the apple in her apron pocket, and her took it out, and the fiddler, he knelt and dug a hole in the grave with his hands, and planted the apple. Then he got up, and they all stood, waiting, and watching, and wondering what would happen.

'A little green shoot come up through the grave, and it growed in front of their eyes, growed to a thin little sapling, growed to a young tree, growed to a tall apple tree with bent and twisted branches. And leaves come out on its branches, all white and turning green. And then the blossom, white and pink. Down the blossom fell, like a shower of snow, and then the apples set, small and green, but swelling and growing rosy. And when the tree was weighed down with its big rosy apples, then the trunk opened like a door, and out stepped the dead girl – alive again! And her was even more beautiful than her had been.

'Well, her mother was crying, and her old Dad was crying – half the people standing round was crying. And the young fiddler, his eyes was wet an' all. But the sisters – there weren't no tears in their eyes. Dry as stones they were.

'So they all went back home, with the girl walking between her old Mom and Dad, and the young fiddler following behind 'cos he couldn't take his eyes off her. And he never did go home – he married the girl. And the people wanted to take the two sisters and drown them for what they'd done, but the girl says, "I'm alive now, and I forgive them, so leave them alone." And the sisters said they was sorry – they said they was – and the people did leave 'em alone.

'And I was at the wedding of the girl and the fiddler, and that's where I heard all this, but when I'd drunk more than enough, I come away.

'Did you hear it? Will you remember it?'

'I have it all noted down, Mrs Riley, and I shall write it down just as you told it to me. But you're tired; you're quite out of breath.'

'I am tired – but you'll come again?'

'I'll come again, Mrs Riley.'

'I've got lots more stories to tell.'

'I promise, I promise,' said Mr Grimsby, as he put his notebook away in his pocket. 'I'll come again.'

## Five

## Another Story from Mrs Naylor

'I was rather afraid, Mrs Naylor, that last time we met we parted on rather bad terms, and I'm sorry for it.'

'Oh, don't you worry about that, Master Grimsby. All forgotten now at any rate. You be sure I'll go and see your Mrs Riley. Take her a few things and all.'

'Oh, if there's anything to be—' Mr Grimsby broke off with a cough, remembering that it had been an offer to pay her for her stories which had offended Mrs Naylor before. 'Well, as you see fit, Mrs Naylor. I shall be taking Mrs Riley a few things too. But I thought she might appreciate a visit from another woman, and she seems to have few friends.'

'I shall see her right, don't you worry. Poor soul,' Mrs Naylor said. 'Poor soul. Would you like a cup of tea, Master Grimsby?'

Master Grimsby knew that tea was expensive for Mrs Naylor to buy, and that when she made it for herself she used the leaves many times over. He knew that, for him, she would use fresh leaves, and he would have liked to have spared her the expense. But he also knew that he would offend her if he made excuses, and that she would enjoy being hospitable and generous. So he said, 'Mrs Naylor, there is nothing I would like more! I am longing for a cup, and I think you will save my life. No sugar, and just a very little milk.'

Mrs Naylor smiled widely, and put the kettle back on the fire. She fetched out her best cups and saucers, emptied her brown platter teapot in the back yard, and set it to warm on the hob. 'Have you ever heard a story called "Foster-father Death", Mr Grimsby?' she asked.

'I don't think I ever have.'

'Well, wait until we've got we tea, and I'll tell it you.'

'Oh,' said Mr Grimsby, feeling in all his pockets. 'Let me get my notebook ready.'

And when the tea was brewed and poured, and when Mr Grimsby was ready with pencil and notebook, Mrs Naylor began to tell the tale.

'There was once a poor man had more childer than he well knowed what to do with. And then another one was born. "I wish," he said, "I wish I could find a good foster-father for this one. Somebody who could afford to set him to a trade and bring him up right." And straight-off, there's a knock at the door. The man answers it, and there's God Hisself standing on the doorstep.

' "I hear you need a foster-father," God says. "Here I am. Hand the baby over."

' "You?" says the poor man. "No fear. I'd never let a

54

son of mine be brought up by You. Look at the way You run the world. The hard-working and honest get nothing but hardship and suffering, and the dishonest and two-faced prosper. Clear off!"

'So God went away with a flea in His ear. But there's another knock, and the poor man answers it, and finds the Devil standing there, with his tail over his arm.

' "Good evening," says the Devil. "I'll take your son and be his foster-father."

' "You're more honest than the last one, I'll give you that," says the poor man. "A bloke knows where he stands with you. But no thanks, Master. I don't like the idea of the kind of trade you might set the little un to. Sling your hook!"

'So the Devil went away. But there's another knock straight after and this time, there's Death standing on the doorstep. "I shall be the child's foster-father," Death says.

' "Come in, Master, come in," says the poor man. "Let's talk about it. You're honest, and fair in your dealings, and I like that. It don't matter if a body's rich or poor, whether they'm handsome or ugly, healthy or sickly, clever or stupid – you deal with 'em all the same."

'So they talk it over, and it's agreed that Death'll take the little un off the poor man's hands, and bring him up, and set him to a trade when he's growed. "And I'm very grateful, Master," says the poor man.

'So Death takes the baby away to his house. It's dark all the time in Death's house, but Death lights it with hundreds and hundreds of candles. More than that. Thousands. They're all the candles of our lives. Everybody alive on Earth has a candle burning in Death's house. And some of 'em burn up good and strong and give a lot of light. Some of 'em are always fluttering and guttering. Some are nearly burned down, and when they burn out, Death goes out from his house to fetch the soul. But there's a candle burning for you and me in Death's house.

'There's nothing to tell of the lad until he's all growed up. Then Death sets him to a trade, like he promised. He makes him a doctor. "This is all you need to know," Death says to him. "When you'm called to somebody sick, look around to see where I am. If I'm standing at the foot of the bed, they'll get better, whatever you do for 'em. But if I'm standing at the head of the bed, say that you're sorry but they won't get better. Because if I'm at the head of the bed, it's their time, and I've come for them, and nothing that you, or any doctor on Earth could do, will save them. Can you remember that?"

' "Easy," said the lad. "Foot of the bed, they'll get better. Head of the bed, they won't."

' "That's all you need to know to become the most famous doctor in the world," Death said. "But, whatever you do, don't ever try to save anybody when I'm standing at their bed head."

' "I won't," said the lad, and away he went into the world, to see what he could do. He got himself a suit of smart dark clothes, and some comfortable lodgings, and he sent out word that he was a doctor. The first time he was called out was to a poor woman who'd been sick for weeks, and her family was worried. But this young doctor comes into her room and all he does is look round. 'Course, he's looking for his foster-father, Death. And even though the woman's so poorly, Death's standing at the foot of the bed, and he's standing at a distance, so the lad knows her'll get better soon. The lad's the only one who can see him; nobody else can. "Keep her warm and feed her well," says the lad. "Her'll be on the mend afore the end of the week. I'll send you my bill." And off he goes with his nose in the air.

'Well, afore the end of the week, the woman's a lot better, and getting better still by the hour. And everybody's talking about the young doctor who only had to look round the room to know what was what.

'So soon, he gets a lot more patients. As soon as he gets into their room, he looks round for Death. Sometimes he's at the foot of the bed, sometimes he's at the head. If he's at the foot, the lad gives his patients tablets made of chalk or sugar, or tells 'em to go and take the air, or eat red meat – it don't matter what he tells 'em to do, because they'm going to get better anyway.

'If Death's standing at the head of the bed, the lad sighs and says he's sorry, but the patient won't get well. If Death's standing at a distance, he says the patient'll live for a day or two, but if Death's standing close, he says, "I'm afraid they won't last the night." And the lad's always right. People go running off to other doctors after he's gone but always, once the lad's said a patient'll die, they die. So the lad becomes a very famous doctor. Everybody wants him to come to them when they'm ill. And the lad gets very rich, and buys hisself a good house, and drives to his patients in a carriage. You'd never have thought he was a poor man's son. That's what come of having Death as a foster-father, see. Death's fair and keeps his promises.

'But then the lad gets called out, and when he gets to the bedside there's a lovely girl lying there. The loveliest thing the lad's ever seen. He looks round the room, and he sees Death standing at the head of the bed. Close by the head of the bed. And the lad's stricken. He can't speak.

'The girl's father and mother are standing by and they can't speak either. They just lean further and further over, looking into his face. He knows what they want him to say. But Death's standing close by the head of the bed.

'So the lad says to the girl's Mom and Dad, "Help me turn the bed round." They think this is a bit funny, but he's the doctor. So they all lay hold of the bed and they turn it right round, so that Death's standing close by the foot. "Her'll be on the mend in an hour or so," says the lad. "Give her lots to drink and keep her warm."

' "Oh thank you, doctor, thank you," they say, and keep saying it, all the way from the bedroom to the door; and then they leave him and run back upstairs to give their daughter lots to drink and keep her warm.

'The lad walks right out of the door into Death's arms,

and Death carries him home, to where all the candles are burning: some of 'em burning high, and some of 'em guttering, and some almost burned out. And Death takes the lad by the arm and he shows him a little end of a candle, burned right down, more melted wax than flame. "That," Death says, "is the girl's candle." And as they watch, the little flame struggles and flickers, dipping into the pool of wax and sputtering and smoking.

‘ "But," says Death, "you have saved her life." And Death takes another candle, a fine big, new candle, and he lights it at the little dying flame just before the candle snuffs out. Death puts the big new candle in place of the old one.

‘ "That's her life now," says Death. "Her'll live as long as the candle burns."

‘ "Thank you, foster-father," says the lad.

‘ "But now I've got one candle too many," says Death, and he looks at the lad.

‘ "Well . . . With so many," says the lad, "does it matter how many there be?"

‘ "Oh aye," says Death. "It matters. I keep strict count. Never one candle too many nor one candle too few. For the light that you saved, another light must be blowed out. Tell me, son, which light shall it be?"

'The lad looked round. So many candles, all through Death's dark house, on every shelf, in every corner. At first he's going to point to one of the old candles that's burned low and is already flickering; but he can't help but think, Why should this old man or old woman be robbed of their

59

last few weeks or days, because of what I did? And then he looks at the tall, new candles, where the flame's hardly caught, and he thinks: They hardly know they're born; they won't miss their life if it's snuffed out . . . But he can't say it. So many candles, half-burned, smoking, smouldering; but at last he turns to Death and says, "Foster-father, which is my candle?"'

'And Death points to a tall, white candle that's hardly begun to burn. The lad picked it up. And blew it out. And that was the end of him.

'Because Death's fair, and Death's honest. He can't be cheated, but he don't cheat. But how would it have turned out, I wonder, if the lad had been raised by God or the Devil?'

'A hard puzzle,' said Mr Grimsby, as he scribbled down the last of the story in his notebook.

'Another cup of tea, Mr Grimsby?'

'Another, yes. And another story if you have one!'

'Oh, stories, stories . . .' She shook her head. 'They don't come into me head nowadays like they used to. I shall enjoy hearing Mrs Riley's. Does her know all the ones I know, I wonder?'

## Six

# Mrs Naylor and Mrs Riley

A fire was burning in the little grate of the range, and the small kitchen was hot. Mr Grimsby, though he was sitting near the door, in the draught, had to mop his face with his handkerchief.

Mrs Riley lay in her bed, and Mrs Naylor sat beside her on a chair, drinking from a cup of what she called 'mazawattie tay', by which she meant tea with whisky in it. She said, 'Do you know this one, Kath? Listen.'

'There was a rich man who had a son, and he wanted this lad to be even richer than he was, and to know things that nobody else knowed. So he sent him off to the Island of Birds, to learn bird-talk. He's away for a year, and when he comes back, his dad says, "Well, what have you learned?" And the son says, "I've learned to see a thing."

' "That all?" says his dad. "Well, I'll send you back for another year, to learn some more."

'So he's away for another year, and when he comes back, it's, "What did you learn, what did you learn?" The lad says, "I learned to see a thing and to hear a thing."

' "No more than that?" says his dad. "Well, I'll give you another year." So off the lad goes again, and his dad can hardly wait for him to get back. Soon as he's through the door, it's, "What did you learn?" The lad says, "I learned to see a thing, hear a thing and understand a thing."

' "Is that all?" says his dad, and starts to wonder if it's all been worth it. He's just thinking this when a chaffinch starts to sing outside the house, and the dad says, "What's that chaffinch saying?"

'The lad listens to it a bit, and then he says, "Oh, nothing much."

' "Well, what?" his dad asks.

' "Oh, nothing that'd interest you," says the lad.

' "Tell me!" his dad says.

' "Oh, you don't want to know," says the lad.

' "Tell me," says his dad, "or you can get out of this house now. I aint spent all this money on your education for nothing."

'So the lad says, "Well, if you must know, the chaffinch said, 'Here sit a father and son side by side, but in time to come, the father will kneel and untie the son's shoes with his teeth, while his mother will wait on him like a serving maid.' That's what the chaffinch said."

'Well, when he hears that, the dad's fit to be tied. Grinding his teeth, he is. Sparks fly. You know that one, Kath?'

'I know how it should go on,' Mrs Riley said. 'The lad's dad was beside himself with thinking how he would have

62

to kneel to his own son. All that I've done for him, he thinks, and I'm to kneel and untie his muddy shoes with my teeth, am I? It'll never happen, he thinks. And he calls to him his servants and he says to 'em, "Take my son away and see that he never grows old. Here's gold," he says, and he gives them gold each. "There'll be more," he says, "when my son has no troubles, and is no trouble, any longer."

'The servants take the gold, and they go off and find the lad, and tell him to come with them down to the seashore and see the ships. And he goes with them, thinking no harm. He's an innocent. And they take him down to the seashore, where it's as lonely as God's first creation, with sand and sea and wind, but nobody to see what happens except the sea-gulls, and nobody but the lad can understand them. And the servants pull out their knives, and they're going to cut the lad's throat, but when he starts begging 'em to let him be, they can't do it. They've got nothing against him, he's a nice lad.

' "But we can't let him go back home," they say. So they take him along the beach until they find a boat. It's a rackety old boat, leaking and rotten, but they strip the lad of his clothes and put him in it. Then they push the boat out to sea until the tide takes it, and they wade back to the beach and wave him bye-bye.

'Next thing, they cut their arms and wipe the blood on the lad's clothes, and they stab their knives through the good weave, and they take the bloody rags back to the lad's dad – terrible waste of good clothes. And the dad gives them more gold and sends 'em away. And he thinks he's safe. When he hears the chaffinch singing, he laughs. "Sing away," he says. "I'll never kneel to my son." '

Mrs Riley was smiling as she told the tale, but she was getting out of breath, so Mrs Naylor took it up.

'Well, there he was in the boat. He drifted and drifted, and water splashed him, and he was wet and cold and hungry, but just as he thought he was going to die, the boat washed up with a bump. The lad clambered out and where was he? He was back on the Island of Birds! So there he stops, listening to the birds all the time, and learning all manner of things off 'em. But he's got hardly anything to eat, and his hair grows long, and a year goes past. He gets thinner and thinner, and his beard grows and another year goes. Now he's so hairy he's like a walking haystack. His own mother wouldn't know him. And another year goes. Three years he's been there, on the island, but before it's made up to four, a ship comes to the island for water, and the Captain takes the lad on board. Well, they couldn't leave him there, could they? He's so hairy and dirty they don't know whether he's old or young, but they cut off his hair and shave his beard and hose him down, and find he's a good-looking young chap underneath it all.

'Now the lad's been listening to the sea-gulls flying round the ship, and he goes to the Captain and he says, "Captain, I understand the birds, and they tell me that some of your crew are pirates, and tomorrow, at midday, they're going to take over the ship, and kill you and the other men."

'Well, the Captain's a bit took aback, but there are some men on board he don't know very well – he had to take 'em on at a foreign port. So he has a word with the men he does know, and the next day, when the pirates attack, the Captain and his men are ready for 'em. And it's the pirates who get the drubbing, and the Captain has 'em tied up, and he brings his ship safe home. He's so pleased with our lad that he takes him home with him, and tells his wife to take good care of him. And that's all I know,' Mrs Naylor said. 'I can't remember what happens to him next.'

'I do,' Mrs Riley said, 'if I've breath to tell it. The lad lived with the Captain and his wife, and was happy with them, and they with him, and he would have been living with them still, except a messenger come to town. This messenger had been sent by the King, and he begun shouting up and down the streets. "His Majesty wishes it known," he said, "as he's been pestered these three years by two ravens who fly about his chimney, screeching fit to part the bricks, so the King can't get any sleep at all; that he wants somebody to come and rid him of these pestilential birds. And anybody who can send 'em packing will be rewarded with half the kingdom and the princess in marriage."—'

'Well, anybody who tries had best get that in writing afore they start, eh, Mr Grimsby?' Mrs Naylor said.

'—People say to the messenger, "Why don't you shoot the ravens?"

'Oh, we've tried,' he says. 'They can't be shot.'

'Why don't you net 'em or lime 'em?'

'Oh, we've tried that; there's no catching them,' says the messenger.

'The lad hears this, and he goes to the Captain and his wife and says, "Thank you for being so good to me; I won't forget you. I'm off to rid the King of these ravens."

' "Don't go," they say. "You always get into trouble, messing with kings." But the lad won't listen, off he goes, all the way to the Royal Palace, and – Oh, I'm out of breath. Can you carry on, Mrs Naylor?'

'That I can't,' Mrs Naylor said. 'I never heard this before. You have a rest and a sup of tea. You getting all this, Mr Grimsby?'

Mr Grimsby was scribbling hurriedly in his notebook. 'All of it, Mrs Naylor, all of it.'

In a while, Mrs Riley was able to go on. 'So, the lad got to the palace, and a very fine palace it was, and he says, "I'm here to get rid of the ravens who're keeping the King awake."

' "Good luck to you," say the guards, and take him to the King.

' "So you think you can rid me of the ravens?" says the King.

' "I can – but will you put in writing that, if I do, I'll

get the princess in marriage and half the kingdom?" says the lad. And the King calls a clerk, and a paper's made up, in black and white, and it's put into the lad's hand. "Right," says the lad, "let me stay in your bedroom tonight, and hear these ravens, and then I'll know what to do."

'So that night the King sleeps on the settle, and the lad sleeps in the Royal Bedroom — and the ravens come, and they scream cracks in the glass, they screech soot down the chimney, they nearly squawk the lad's ears off his head. But he listens to 'em all night. And the next day, when the King wants to know what he's going to do, he says:

' "It's what you're going to do that matters, King. I listened to what the ravens was saying, and they was talking about the famine of three years ago — you remember it, King?"

' "I do," says the King. "The poor were making a dreadful fuss, dreadful."

' "Birds went hungry as well as people," says the lad. "These ravens that keep you awake now, were on their nest then, trying to hatch three eggs. There was only a week to go to the hatching when the hen-raven was so starved, poor thing, that she had to leave them to go and find something to eat. The cock-raven hadn't been able to find enough food to keep her fed. The cock came back and found the eggs going cold, so he sat on them himself, and while he was sitting on 'em, two of the eggs hatched — but one of the chicks died. Then the hen came back, and she tried to hatch the last egg, but it was no good, it was cold, and it would no more hatch than a boiled egg. So then, King, the hen-raven said she'd take the one live chick with her, because she'd laid the egg and it was hers. But the cock said that she left the nest, and all the chicks would have died if it hadn't been for him – so the chick must go with him. And they've been fighting over this ever since. They've come to you for justice, King. That's what they've been screaming about round your chimney. They want you to decide which one has the right to the chick. So give justice, King – and then give me my wife and my kingdom!"

'Well, the King puts his head on one side, and then on the other side. He pulls his lip and picks his nose and thinks of this and thinks of that and then he says to the lad, "What would you say?"

' "It's for you to say," says the lad. "You're the King."

'So the King, he thinks some more and makes up his mind; and when the ravens come and start screeching that night, the King shouts up the chimney, "My judgement is: the cock-raven has the right of it!"—'

'Tcha! Might have knowed,' Mrs Naylor said. 'One bloke deciding for another and never mind what the woman suffered! Always the same.'

'—"I decide for the cock," says the King, and the cock-raven flies off. But the hen-raven stays to fly round and round the chimney, widdershins – against the sun. And

68

that's a raven-curse. Her was cursing the King for his judgement—'

'And good for her,' said Mrs Naylor.

'—But the ravens never come back, and the King gets his first night's sleep in three years. So, the next day, he gives half his kingdom to the lad, and marries him to the princess – but the marriage is no sooner over than the King drops dead – because of the raven's curse – and so the lad becomes King of the whole country. And a very good King he is – and he doesn't forget the Captain and his wife.'

And Mrs Riley lay back, very much out of breath. Mrs Naylor asked her if she wanted another cup of tea, but she shook her head.

'That's not the end of the story,' Mrs Naylor said. 'We haven't heard about the chaffinch yet. No, let's see, there's our lad, married to the princess – but nobody asked the princess if she wanted to be married to him, did they? And her baint very happy about it. So her decides to get rid on him, and her brings him a cup of wine one day, that her's put poison in. And he drinks it and straightaway his skin turns – he's a leper. And the people say, "We don't want a leper for a King—"'

' "—It would bring the country bad luck," ' Mrs Riley said.

'So the lad puts on a cloak, and a bell round his neck to warn folk he's coming, and away he goes like a beggar, out on his ear, out of luck, down on his uppers. Got nothing to show for being King.'

69

'Oh, I know what happens then, I know,' said Mrs Riley. 'There was a screeching and a cawing, and a big black raven flew down, and it was the same cock-raven as had flown round the King's chimney. "You helped me, so I'll help you," says the raven. "I know how you can cure yourself and be as good as ever you were – you must wash yourself all over in the blood of a child."

' "What?" says the lad. "That I can never do. If I must be a leper and an outcast, then so be it – but never will I murder an innocent to save my own skin."

' "No murder, no murder," says the raven. "Because at the world's end there's a well, and the water of that well – even just the splash of one drop of it – can bring the dead back to life. And I shall fly to that well and bring the water back in my beak, and it'll be as if the child had a few moment's peaceful sleep."

' "Oh," said the lad. "Then I'll do it."

'So on they went together, with the raven riding on the lad's shoulder, until they come to a house where all the neighbours was standing outside, and some of the women was crying. They wouldn't let the lad come near, because he was a leper, but he called to them and asked what was wrong. "Oh," they said, "there's a child in the house that's sick and dying fast."

' "Then let me through," says the lad. "I might be a leper now, but I used to be a doctor, and I can cure the child maybe."

'Some said, no, he'd make the child worse, but the

70

child's mother come running out and said if the Devil Himself offered to cure her child, her'd let him try. So the lad and the raven went into the house, and the lad said that everyone must leave, or his magic wouldn't work. And nobody wanted to stay near a leper, so they all went out. Off flies the raven through the window, away to the world's end and the well. The lad takes off all his clothes, and takes his knife from his belt and bends over the sick child in the bed. But he can't do it, and he throws down his knife and sits by his clothes . . .

'But then the raven comes back to the window-sill,' said Mrs Naylor, 'and there's water dribbling from its beak. "Now or never," says the lad to hisself, and he takes his knife again, and gets up, and cuts the child's throat. Out comes the thick blood, out comes the thin, and the lad washes in it, rubs it over his face, over his arms, over his belly and legs and back, and everywhere the blood touches or runs, his skin heals, and when he's finished, he's twice as handsome as he was before. And then the raven flies over the bed and drops the water on the child, and the child comes back to life and sits up and yells for its Mom.

'In runs its mother, and in comes everybody else, and they'm a bit put out to see the lad standing there starkers – but the child's better, when it was dying before, so they forgive him. They think it's a miracle that he's not a leper any more, and they give him some clothes, and some money to help him on his way. So the lad says goodbye, and thanks, to the raven, and off he goes back to the palace, where all the people are glad to see him back, and make him King again – but what about the princess, who poisoned him? What happens to her?'

'Put her in a barrel with spikes on the inside and roll her downhill,' said Mrs Riley. 'The nasty little cat.'

'Oh, now, Kath, that's not like you. Poor wench. Her didn't want to marry him.'

'Her didn't have to poison him,' Mrs Riley said.

Mrs Naylor said, 'Mr Grimsby: what do you think should happen to the princess?'

'Just a moment.' Mr Grimsby frowned as his hand hurried over the paper. Then he sat back in his chair, and eased his cramped fingers. 'It was unkind of the princess, indeed, to poison the lad with leprosy but, as Mrs Naylor says, her wishes hadn't been considered . . . I think it a trifle harsh to put her in a barrel with spikes on the inside. A Christian forgiveness would be best, I think.'

'A *Christian* forgiveness?' said Mrs Naylor. 'Oh, I think we'd better fetch up the barrel, after all!'

'Oh, now, now, Mrs Naylor,' said Mr Grimsby.

'Oh, who cares anyway,' said Mrs Naylor. 'We've got to get on. Let's just say they packed the wench out the palace gates and her went off and was never seen again.'

'Say that then, all right,' Mrs Riley agreed.

'Then her can go and make her own ending,' Mrs Naylor said. 'Her might have come to a bad end, or her might have lived happy ever after. You can take your pick.'

'All right,' said Mrs Riley.

'Anyway, our lad's King again, and he starts thinking about his old mom and dad, who sent him away because of what the chaffinch said. And he sends a messenger to his old dad, saying, "Get everything ready, because the King is coming to visit you."

'And the old Dad gets in a fright and he sends a message back, saying, "I'm too poor, I can't have a King visiting me. I've got nowhere to put him up, nothing to feed him." But the lad sends back saying, "The King is coming."

'So the lad goes to visit his old Mom and Dad, and he finds 'em so poor, he's shocked. They've done badly since he was away, and they'm living in an old shed, dressing in rags, with hardly a farthing to scratch theirselves with. Up comes the lad, in his coach, with soldiers and trumpets, and all dressed in gold. His old Mom and Dad don't know him – well, they'm on their knees, they hardly dare look him in the face. And the lad says to 'em, "You poor people," he says, "haven't you got a son to look after you?"

' "Oh no," says the old man. "We had a son but he – well, he died," he says.

'But it's late, it's night, and the King says, "I've had a long journey, show me where I'm to sleep." And the old couple show him their bed, which is a disgrace, with hardly a rag on it. But they've still got their manners, the old couple, so the old man goes in to ask the King if he needs anything.

' "I need a bit of help," says the King. "There's a terrible knot in the lace of this shoe. I can't get it undone," he says.

So the old man has a go, but he can't undo it either. And he gets down on his knees, and puts his teeth to the knot, to get it undone. And just as he's doing that, in comes the old woman, carrying a basin of water and some towels over her arm, for the King to wash in.

' "Oh, Mother! Oh, Father!" says the lad. "The chaffinch spoke true!"

'And the old couple look him in the face and see who he is – and it was half an hour before they stopped dancing. But then the old man says, "I tried to have you killed, my own son. I deserve everything that's happened since. I deserve more. I should be put in a barrel with spikes on the inside and rolled downhill."

' "Oh, that's too much trouble," says the lad. "Where would I get a barrel with spikes on the inside at this time of night? Let's just forget it, and you come to the palace and live with me." So they did, and when they got to the palace, they had a great feast.

'I myself walked a thousand miles to be there. I drunk beer and wine and whisky, and when the feast was over they give me a big piece of cake to take home and a horse made of ice to ride on; and its saddle was carved from a turnip, and its reins was made of peas strung on a string. So off I rode; but half-way home I stopped to rest, but I fell asleep – and pigs come out of the woods and et the turnip saddle, and chickens come and et the reins of peas. And

74

then the sun rose and melted me horse away, so when I woke, I had to walk. And as I was walking a pigeon called out of the wood, "You fool you, you fool you!" And I thought it was shouting at me, so I throwed me piece of cake at it in a temper – and I come home no better off than I left.'

Mrs Riley sighed. Mr Grimsby scribbled for some moments longer and then said, 'I have it! I have it all.'

Mrs Naylor said. 'No, no . . . If he can forgive his dad, he ought to forgive the princess an' all, and fetch her back to the palace. After all, it's her palace.'

'Her loves the lad, really,' said Mrs Riley, 'and when her thinks he's dead of leprosy, her breaks her heart and dies.'

'No, no,' said Mrs Naylor. 'It's not her who gives him leprosy at all. There's a servant who's in love with her, and when her marries the lad, *he* puts the poison in the lad's drink – and then *he* marries the princess while the lad's away . . . And when the lad's cured and he comes back, he kills the servant – let's put *him* in the barrel with spikes on the inside – and the princess is happy to have the lad back, and they live happy ever after. *That's* the way to tell it.'

'Don't forget the lad going back to his mom and dad.'

'Oh, that an' all, that an' all,' Mrs Naylor said, standing up and drawing her shawl over her head. 'I shall have to be off, Kath. Don't you fret, I shall be back tomorrow. Goodbye each.'

And she went away.

# Seven

# The Churchyard Grim's Story

The walk home from Sergeant Lamb's was often steep, and Mr Grimsby, not as young as he once was, often stopped to rest and breathe hard. He would stand and look about him, and pat his pocket to make sure he still had his little notebook safe. Behind him, if he turned and looked, was the town, raising its clamour of hammers and metal into the sky yet, though dusk was coming. As the sun's light faded from the sky, it had begun to be replaced by the red glow of foundry fires.

He turned again and started on his road home. Here were fields and hedges, and the hills hid from him the fires and din of other towns. And here was the little, square, grey church of St Thomas, with its tall gate of grey, grooved wood, grown over green with moss. Crowded in its little churchyard, among the yew trees were, he knew, the graves of some of Cromwell's troopers, killed in local scuffles, and also of his own great-grandparents. A pleasant place to take another rest, he thought, and leaned against the low wall of grey and green and ochre stones, and

77

looked at the leaning gravestones, their words turned green by moss, or worn smooth.

The sun had been sinking below the western hills, its rim burning on the edge of the hill like a beacon fire, and turning the sky red above it. The sun sank and vanished, and darkness gathered quickly. Darkness seemed to rise from among the gravestones, to come ducking out from under the low-hanging branches of the yew. Mr Grimsby looked down his road home, and saw it dwindling, fading in darkness. He heaved himself up from the wall and started on his way again.

From the north side of the churchyard came trotting a dog, a big dog, and it fell in at his side. It was a black and shaggy dog, large of head and large of paw, and its back stood as high as Mr Grimsby's broad waist. It looked up at him in the dusk, and its eyes caught the fading light and gleamed red.

'Hello, boy,' said Mr Grimsby to the dog. 'What a fine fellow you are, aren't you?'

'I'll see you home,' said the dog.

Mr Grimsby stopped short and looked about him to see who had spoken. There was no one near except the dog.

'A story to shorten the way, since you're a man for stories,' said the dog. 'What story shall it be?'

'You – you know stories?' Mr Grimsby asked.

'Many a one, many a one,' said the dog.

'I would – well, I would be honoured to hear a story from you,' said Mr Grimsby.

'I'll tell you a story about a land where all the animals say, "Good day!"

'It starts with a lad who made his living by hunting and killing – birds and hares he killed. Well, anybody might do that. But he hunted foxes and weasels and cats as well – I daresay he would have hunted dogs if there'd been money in it. It's all money with men.

'Well, he used to go off into the wilds, and he built hisself a hut out there, and there he lived – but winter come early one year, and he was snowed in. Not that he was troubled too much. He had wood for his stove, and the hut was by a lake where the birds come, so he didn't think he'd starve. He had lines of ducks hanging from his ceiling, ready for the eating.

'But he got a fright when somebody rattled at his door. He pulled the door open and peered out, and there, in the darkness and the cold wind, was sitting a big red fox. "As you love your life," says the fox, "let me in before I freeze to death."

'So the lad opens the door more and lets the fox come in, and in it come, with snow falling from its fur. Straight to the fire it went and lay down, and sees the ducks hanging from the ceiling. "As you love to eat," says the fox, "give me one of them ducks. I haven't eaten for three days, and me belly thinks me throat's cut."

'The lad got down one of the ducks and give it to the fox, who soon left nothing of it but the feathers, beak and legs. When it had finished, the fox wrapped its tail round its feet, grinned at the lad, and says, "Thanks. You'll be glad you did me this favour – I'm the King of all the Foxes, and I'll see that you're rewarded."

'The lad smiled, but he took no mind. He didn't think a fox could do much for him, even if it was a king.

'They lived together happily enough for a day or two, and then there come another rattling at the door. The lad opened it a crack, and then slammed it shut. "A wolf!" he said to the fox.

'From the other side of the door, in the dark and cold, the wolf howled. "As you love your life," it said, "let me in, before I freeze to death."

' "Let him in," says the fox to the lad, "but tell him not to look up." Because all these ducks were hanging from the ceiling.

'The lad opened the door again. "You can come in, and welcome, if you promise never to look up."

' "I promise, I promise!" says the wolf.

'So the lad pulled open the door and let the wolf in, and the wolf went straight to the fire to warm itself. Melted snow ran from its fur in streams. But as soon as it was warm, the wolf looked up and saw the ducks. "Ah!" it says. "Boy, as you love your belly, give me one of those ducks."

'The fox was angry. "You promised you wouldn't look up!"

' "I'm the King of all the Wolves," says the wolf, "and I look where I please. But give me a duck, besides shelter here, and I'll see that you're rewarded."

'The lad was afraid to refuse the wolf, and got a duck down for it, but he didn't think there was anything a wolf could do to reward him.

'Then there come a great thudding at the door, that frightened them all. The lad went and looked through the latch-hole, and jumped back as if he'd been shot. "A bear!" he says.

'From outside the bear roars, "Let me in, as you love your life, before I freeze to death!"

' "Don't let it in!" says the wolf.

' "No, let it in," says the fox, "but make it promise not to look up."

'So the lad shouts, "Don't think I'm on my own! I've got the King of the Foxes and the King of the Wolves here with me. And we'll let you in, if you promise that you'll not look up!"

' "I promise!" shouts the bear.

'So the lad opens the door, and the bear comes shouldering in, filling half the hut and making for the fire. And he looks up, sees the ducks and says, "Give me one of them!"

' "You promised you wouldn't look up!" says the fox.

' "How can I not look up?" says the bear. "Besides, I'm the King of all the Bears, and I'll reward you – if you save me from hunger now."

'How can you refuse a bear, even if it isn't a King? The lad got down three ducks and gave them to the bear, who ate them all.

'And then an eagle banged its beak on the door and screamed to be let in, and it had to be given a duck, and it was the King of Eagles; and then a hare scratched at the door and squealed to be let in, and the lad had to find some of the oats he had left for it, and it was grateful. It was the King of Hares.

'The lad asked the others to promise not to eat the hare, and they all promised that they wouldn't.

' "Will you keep that promise better than the one about looking up?" the lad asks, and they said they would. But the hare usually sat on the lad's lap, or was carried about in his pocket.

'So they passed the winter together. The lad and the fox would hunt birds on the frozen lake. The bear, who was strong, would drag home trees for firewood. The wolf and the eagle would range, and try and catch hares – and the little King of Hares would stay home and keep the fire in. In the evenings they sat by the fire and told stories – fox stories, wolf stories, bear stories, eagle stories, hare stories and lad stories. Wonderful stories were told by that hearth! – and so the winter went by, and the good weather come again, and the fox, the wolf, the bear, the eagle and the hare could all go back to the wilds.

' "But what reward shall we give the lad for his hospitality?" the fox asks. "We must give him something, we promised him something."

' "There's no need to give me anything," says the lad.

' "Would you like," the fox asks, "the Emperor's daughter for a wife?"

' "Would the Emperor's daughter want me?" the lad asks.

'But the wolf, and the bear, and the eagle and the hare all said, "Yes, oh yes! The Emperor's daughter for our lad!"

'The lad laughed and said, "The Emperor's daughter lives miles from here, in a great palace, where her father keeps her locked up! How would I ever meet her, let alone get her to love me?"

' "Leave that to me," says the fox. "Give me a day or two. I'll think about it."

'And the wolf, the bear, the eagle and the hare all stayed on with the lad while the fox prowled about on his own, thinking. And then the fox called them all together.

' "Bear," says the fox, "we shall need a log. And you, my lad, must take your axe and shape it something like one of your ploughs."

'The bear fetched a big log from the forest, and the lad took his axe and shaped it, as near as he could remember, like a plough. "Now," says the fox, "you stay here, my lad, and look after yourself, because we shall be back. Bear, you carry the plough. And the rest of you, come on."

'And off they all went, on the long journey to the Emperor's palace, leaving the lad behind. He felt lonely, after spending all the winter in good company, and he hoped that the fox, nor the bear, nor the wolf nor the eagle would eat the little hare.

'The fox, the wolf, the bear – carrying the plough – and the hare travelled across the land, up and down hill, over streams, over rivers, over grass and stone. The eagle flew ahead and found them the way. And they come to the Emperor's palace.

'The hare was the smallest. The hare slipped under the gate, and opened it from the inside, and let the others in. Then the bear was ploughman and pushed the plough over the palace lawn, and the wolf and the fox walked ahead, as if they were pulling it. This was the fox's plan, and he'd told it to them all as they travelled. Backwards and forwards they went, across the lawn, ploughing it. The eagle flew overhead.

'The people in the palace saw them, and stared, and ran and fetched more people to stare. And the Emperor was told, and he come to the balcony to look, and he sent for his Queen, and she sent for her daughter, the princess; and they all stood on the balcony and watched the ploughing.

'Down flew the eagle, snatched up the princess and carried her off.

' "Run!" says the fox, and the hare and the fox and the wolf and the bear all run through the palace gate and away as fast as they could.

'They met up a way off, and the fox explained to the princess that he was taking her to meet a fine young lad, who would make her a good husband.

' "I think I'd rather go home," she says.

' "Oh no, no, no," says the fox. "This is a grand lad,

good-hearted, a fine hunter, and as beautiful as you are, my love."

'The princess began to be a little curious and she says, "Where does he live?"

' "You'll see that when we get there," says the fox.

' "Is it far?"

' "Well, what's far to me might not be far to you," says the fox.

' "I'll come," says the princess. "I'll meet him – but I'm not saying I'll marry him."

' "No more you should, as yet," says the fox; and they travelled on, with the princess riding on the bear's back.

'They got to the hunter's hut by the lakeside, and pretty it looked in the summer, but the princess had never seen so poor a place, so dirty, so rough. "I can't live here!" she says.

' "Stay a while," says the fox. "You'll get to love it."

'And then the fox barked, and the wolf howled; the bear whooped, the eagle screamed and the hare squealed, and from behind the hut came the lad, who'd been chopping wood. His shirt was off, because of the heat, and sweat and grime were running down his chest; his face was red and his hair damp and messed; and his trousers and old wooden shoes were grubby and worn and not at all in the fashion. The princess turned her face away.

' "Oh poo!" she says. "I can't love him."

' "Give him a chance," says the fox. "Get him cleaned up, and you'll soon see his finer side."

'And when the lad had washed and put on his other shirt, he certainly looked a lot more handsome – but looks aren't everything, and his voice was rough, and his hut small and dusty, with bare wooden floors and bare wooden walls, and nothing but hard wooden benches and stools to sit on. And the food he served was nothing but hard bread and half-burned meat, and nothing to drink but water. It was too dreadful. "Oh, take me home," says the princess. "I could never live here."

' "Give it a month," says the fox. "See a little of life. Give the lad a hand – fetch in the water for him. If you still don't like it after a month, we'll take you home again."

'So the princess stayed a month, and she found out that a little dust and dirt doesn't kill, and that the lad, though he was shy with her, could say some clever and funny things sometimes, and knowed how to do more things than her'd ever thought on – catch fish, clean them, cook them; mend roofs, chop wood, find mushrooms and berries, sew, mend shoes – there seemed to be nothing he couldn't do. And her found that her could do some of these things herself, if her tried. At the end of the month, her said her thought her'd stop a bit longer afore her went home. The lad was glad to hear it, because by this time he was daft about her.

'What they none of them knowed was that the Emperor was searching for his daughter. He was sending men all up and down the country, and one of them found her, living with the lad, and told her that her father wanted her to come back to the palace.

' "In a while," her says. "Not just yet. I'm enjoying myself here."

'The messenger rode back to the palace and told the Emperor what his daughter had said. The Emperor wasn't pleased. He called for the General of his army. "General," he says, "take your heavy troops, take your light troops; take the cavalry, take the infantry – and bring my daughter back!"

'The army marched, in their red and in their blue and green; the heavy and the light, the infantry and the cavalry. The eagle, flying high, saw them coming and flew to warn the fox.

' "Friends!" says the fox. "Now's the time to call on our subjects!"

'The bear roared, the fox barked, the wolf howled, the eagle screamed, the hare shrieked – and from all sides, from the forests, from the moors, come running foxes, and wolves, and bears and hares. From all sides come eagles flying.

'The fox formed them up into a great army and they fell on that of the Emperor. The foxes and the wolves attacked on one flank, snarling and biting; and then the eagles flew in from the other side, dropping rocks; and the bears, with their great strength, come in behind the eagles. The hares, who weren't good at fighting, made theirselves useful by carrying the orders of General Fox about the battlefield.

'The Emperor's troops broke and run, all the way home to the Emperor. When the Emperor was told that his troops had been scattered by wolves and foxes, bears and eagles, he says, "So! Witchcraft! Then I too shall use witchcraft!" And he sent for the most skilful witches of his empire.

' "My soldiers have failed to bring me back my daughter," he says. "So I want you to do it. And I want you to bring back this swine her's living with an' all. I've things to say to him!"

'The witches listened to all the Emperor could tell them of his daughter. They listened to all the soldiers could tell them of the place where the princess was. And then two of the witches stood up. One, a woman, said, "I shall bring back the princess."

' "And I," says the man-witch, "shall bring back the man."

'So off the witches flew – in barrels. The witch had an old brandy cask, and the man-witch flew in a barrel that had once held salted herring. The witch landed her brandy-cask near the hunter's hut, gathered up the trinkets her'd brought with her, and went up to the house, where her found the princess at the well, fetching water. The princess' hair was tied up in tidy plaits, her had a sack tied over her dress for an apron, and wooden shoes on her feet.

' "Do you want to buy, do you want to buy?" calls out the old witch, and held up the lace and ribbons and necklaces her carried.

'The princess smiles. "I haven't any money."

' "Come and look anyway, my love. There's no harm in looking."

'So the princess sits down with the witch by the well, and her looked at ribbons and rings, and brooches and lace, and necklaces and shoe-buckles. "But where have you come from?" her asked the witch. "No one lives for hundreds of miles around!"

' "I live in a barrel," says the witch.

' "A barrel!"

' "A brandy-cask, my dear. I flew here in it. I left it just over there."

' "Oh! I don't believe you!" says the princess.

' "Come and see, then," says the witch, and her led the princess by the hand to the place where her'd left her barrel. "It's much bigger inside than it looks," says the witch. "Why, it's a little palace once you're inside!"

' "I don't believe you," says the princess.

' "Crawl in and see."

'So the princess crawled in and, as soon as her was inside, the witch clapped her hands, called out her magic words – and into the air rose the barrel and away it flew, back to the Emperor's castle with the princess inside it.

'And what of the man-witch and our lad? Well, the lad was harder to catch than the princess, because nobody had ever bowed and scraped and made their living by being nice to *him*. So he knew that when somebody smiles and behaves all sweet and kind, it isn't always because they

89

mean you well. So the man-witch left his barrel near the hut, and went down to the lake where he found the lad fishing. "Quick! Quick!" he cried. "Your princess is being stuffed in a barrel and taken from you!"

'The lad jumped up and stared. "Who are you?" he says.

' "Quick! Quick! If you want to save your princess!" says the man-witch.

'And the lad, because he was daft about the princess, run back to the hut without asking any more questions, even though he thought it was very strange, the way that stranger had turned up from nowhere. And he saw the barrel lying on its side by the hut. "Her's inside it, her's inside it!" cried the man-witch, panting up behind.

'Down on his hands and knees went the lad and into the barrel he crawled – and the witch clapped his hands, and sang out, and the barrel twitched upright, sprang into the air and flew away with the lad inside it, away to the Emperor's palace.

'So two barrels landed in the courtyard of the Emperor's palace, but they got very different welcomes. The brandy-cask was surrounded by a guard of honour, and the Emperor and his Empress were there to meet it. The princess was lifted out, and her mother tut-tutted over her hair, and apron and wooden shoes. Her was led away to her private rooms, to be washed and dressed and made to look like an Emperor's daughter again.

'Soldiers also surrounded the herring barrel, when it landed – but they dragged the lad out by his hair and by his

collar, and they led him away to a dark prison under-
ground. There they threw him, and there they locked
him, and there they left him until such time as they could
hang him.

'The princess wept when her heard. Her begged them
to let him go, but the Emperor said it was impossible. So
the princess argued, her screamed, her throwed things, her
held her breath, her ripped her frock, her refused to eat,
her refused to speak until they let the lad go. But the
Emperor wouldn't talk to her and the Empress only give
her a look and said, "Well, *really*, my dear."

'So there was the lad in the dungeon, waiting to be
hung, and the princess lying on her bed, refusing to eat or
speak. A nice fix.

'It was lucky for the lad and the princess that the animals
were busy. A little bird flew to the princess' windowsill, at
the top of a tall tower, hopped there and flirted its tail, and
then flew to her bedpost and looked at her. And when her
opened her eyes and looked at it – away it flew, out of the
window and back to its commander, the eagle.

' "The princess lives, her lives, her lives," sang the bird,
"but has cried herself thin. At the top of the tower her
lives, her weeps, her fades."

'Another little bird flew to the little barred window at
the very bottom of a castle tower, and looked down into
the deep blackness of the dungeon. Through the bars the
bird hopped, and flew down into the cell, and landed on
the head, and then on the knee, of the lad, who sprawled

91

down there, in the darkness and the filth. And then away flew the little bird, back up to the window and through the bars into the light, and away through the air to its commander, the eagle.

' "The lad's still alive, he lives, he lives, but starved thin, and sick and sad, and Death calls his name."

'And a hawk that had hovered above the palace come and said, "The gallows are built, the noose is hung."

'The eagle told all this to the fox, and the fox said, "No longer can we wait – call your people! Call the bears, call the eagles, call the hares, call the wolves – and I shall call the foxes!".

'And the army of the animals marched on the Emperor's palace.

'The Emperor thought he was safe behind his high palace walls, and he give the order for the lad to be brought out from the dungeon, and for the princess to be dragged from her bed to the balcony of her room, so that her could watch the lad hang.

'Soldiers marched the lad up the dungeon steps and into the bright light. He was dazzled after his time in the dungeon, but his hands were tied behind him, so he couldn't shade his eyes. His guard dragged him up the steps of the platform. All around the platform stood the Emperor's regiments, and the palace servants. High above, on her balcony, the princess leaned down and stared at her lad, for this was the last her'd ever see on him. But he couldn't see her, because, after his time in the dungeon, he couldn't see in the bright light.

'Then, flying high over the palace walls, come eagles, hundreds and hundreds of eagles! And in their talons they carried hares! Each eagle carried two hares.

'Down the eagles swept, and dropped the hares in the palace yard. The yard was rippling like water with the scores of little grey, furry hares, all running for the gates! And, afore the soldiers could move, the eagles flew in their faces, screaming and scratching with their talons!

'To the gates run the hares, in squads, and up on each other's shoulders they hopped and climbed, until the hare at the top was high enough to open the gates – and not a soldier tried to stop them, because the soldiers were too busy fighting the eagles.

'In through the gates come the bears, hordes of fierce bears, companies of snarling, clawing bears, who seized soldiers and hugged them until they fainted. And still the eagles flew down from above with their sharp beaks and their sharp talons and their screams. And now the hares run about the soldiers' feet, tripping them up.

'In come the wolves, in come the foxes, and they run for the platform where the lad stood, with his hands tied behind him, and the noose about his neck. Up on the platform they went, a grey stream of wolves, and a red stream of foxes. To the left and the right they bit and nipped, until, to get away from them, the soldiers jumped off the platform into the arms of the bears. And the King of the Foxes reared up on his hind legs, and bit through the ropes that tied the lad's hands, and the lad was able to take the noose from around his own neck.

'Up flew the King of the Eagles to the princess' balcony, and it lifted her in its talons, and flew down with her, and set her beside the lad on the platform. So the lad was able to put his arms around her, and her put her arms round him.

'The soldiers and the servants all fled away, out through the open gates, running for all they was worth from the bears, and the wolves and the foxes. And the Emperor and the Empress were brought, by a guard of wolves, before the council of the animal kings. There, on the scaffold, sat the King of Foxes, the King of Bears, the King of Wolves, the King of Eagles, and the King of Hares.

' "Come and sit with us, lad," says the King of Foxes. "Be the King of Men, and let us hold trial on the prisoners."

'So the lad come, hand in hand with his princess, and they sat between the hare and the wolf.

' "What crime are the prisoners accused of?" cried the clerk of the court, who was a fox.

' "The prisoners stand accused of hunting and killing the birds of the air," said the prosecutor, who was a wolf, "of hunting and killing the hare-people; of hunting and killing the fox-people, of hunting and killing the wolf-people, of hunting and killing bear-people; of seeking the death of our friend, the lad, and of tormenting their own child."

' "Will any defend them?" asked the fox-king.

' "I will," says the princess. "They were not always bad to me."

'But, try as her might, her couldn't deny the prisoners' crimes, and when the fox called for a verdict, the eagles screamed, the bears roared, the wolves howled, the foxes barked, the hares shrieked, the one word, "Guilty!"

' "What shall their punishment be?" asks the fox-king.

' "They shall be hunted and torn to pieces," says the prosecuting wolf, and all the animals agreed.

' "No, no!" cried the princess. "Be merciful, though they were not – spare them!"

'And the lad, because he saw his princess was unhappy, knelt to the fox-king and said, "Spare them, please." He stood beneath the great paw of the bear and said, "Let them live, for my princess' sake." He turned to the wolf, the hare, the eagle. "Be merciful, great ones, we beg you."

' "Man, woman," says the fox-king to the Emperor and Empress, "we will spare your lives on these conditions – that you give up all your claims to rule, that you kneel to our lad here and call him King, and that you leave this land forever."

'The princess' mother and father, trembling, knelt to all the animals, and the lad, and their daughter, and agreed to it all. And they was escorted from that country by a guard of wolves and bears, and they never dared return.

'Some of the people did, some of the servants, some of the farmers and weavers, cobblers, dyers, potters, and all those other useful people. But they returned to find that

95

the new Emperor, the High King of all the country, was a fox, and the new Empress a vixen! And under his rule was the King of men, the hunting lad, and the Queen of women, the princess – and a King and Queen of wolves, a King and Queen of eagles, a King and Queen of bears, a King and Queen of hares – and of cats, and mice, and sheep and snakes, and dogs and bats – Oh, the list is long. And they all met together in a great council, whenever there was anything to decide.

'And this is true, this country exists, though very far away. The prime minister is a donkey, and the chancellor a magpie; the archbishop's a wolf, and the Minister for War an ass, though many of the regiments are made up of bears and lions. All of the judges are bats. So, you see, it goes on as well as any other country.

'There many men and women pull carts, while shops are kept by hares and badgers. Men and women catch rats, and cats teach school. Horses ride in dog-carts, rats are bankers, and men and women vote for pigs, toads and snakes.

'That's the land where all the animals say, "Good day!" And now we, too, must say "good day," Mr Grimsby. I can go with you no further.'

With something of a start, Mr Grimsby stopped listening to the story and looked about him. They stood before a tall door, with a great brass knocker, and an iron foot-scraper beside it.

'Where is this?' Mr Grimsby asked. 'I don't know this place.'

'No,' said the dog. 'But you'll come to know it.'

'But I must go home,' Mr Grimsby said, and turned to leave the strange door – but behind him was nothing but the utmost darkness. Not the friendly darkness of lane and bush and field when the sun has gone down, but the harsh blackness of emptiness, void, nothing. Mr Grimsby's voice shook as he asked again, 'Where are we?'

'At the end of the world,' said the dog. 'That is Heaven's Door. Knock, and they'll let you in.'

Mr Grimsby turned and looked at the door again – and he looked at the big dog – and at the door. 'How—? I say . . . I mean . . . Is—?'

'It's Heaven's Door,' said the dog, 'and now I leave you.'

And the big black dog, the Churchyard Grim, trotted back along the road they had travelled, back to Earth, back to his church, where, in the last darkness of the night, he slipped again into his own grave in the north side of the churchyard.

To meet the Black Dog, the Moddy Doo, Trash, Padfoot, the Churchyard Grim, means that your death will follow soon.

## Eight

# Another Tale from Sergeant Lamb

After the black dog left him, Mr Grimsby turned and saw that he was not alone, as he'd thought. A crowd of people were gathered at Heaven's Door, all waiting to be let in. There were people of every kind: mothers holding babies, small children alone, people naked and people in work-clothes, people dressed for weddings, and people in nightshirts.

Mr Grimsby stood among them for a while; and then he said, 'Has anyone knocked?'

'We've all knocked,' said a woman beside him. 'Nobody comes.'

'I've been waiting an age,' said a man, and, to be sure, he was wearing strange, old-fashioned clothes, such as Mr Grimsby had never seen worn in his lifetime.

'Dear me!' Mr Grimsby said. 'I expected better service in Heaven!'

He felt a hand on his shoulder and, turning, found Sergeant Lamb standing behind him. 'I thought I knowed that voice,' said the old soldier. 'Fancy meeting you here!'

'You didn't think I'd go to the other place, I hope!' said Mr Grimsby.

'No, but I thought I might,' said the Sergeant. 'Has anybody knocked at the door?'

'Aye!' – 'Yes!' – 'Ar!' cried several people all at once. 'We've all knocked – D'you think we're fools? Nobody comes.'

'We'll just have to wait then,' said the Sergeant. 'And we haven't even got a drink or a pouch of tobacco between we all! There's a pity.' Looking at Mr Grimsby, he added, 'If you was still collecting stories, I could tell you one to pass the time.'

Mr Grimsby reached into his breast-pocket. 'I've still got my notebook and my pencil.' He found a clean page, and licked his pencil's point. 'I'm always glad to hear a story. If your jaw's in good trim, Sergeant—'

The Sergeant, looking about at those people nearest him, saw that they were ready to be entertained too. 'Well . . . I know a good un about a funeral . . .

'There was this old woman, see, who died, and her left three daughters and one necklace of amber beads. Beautiful thing. Every bead like a drop of honey.

'Well, which sister was to have the necklace?

' "We'll have a contest," says eldest. "Winner gets the beads."

' "A baking contest," says middle sister, a'cos her was a champion baker.

' "A knitting contest," says youngest, a'cos her could knit in her sleep.

' "Neither one," says eldest. "We shall have a fair contest, where we all start equal. Now, we all have husbands, don't we?"

'The other two nods.

' "And they'm all as daft as one another," says eldest.

'The other two nods harder.

' "Then the one who wins the beads'll be," says eldest, "the one who makes the biggest fool on her husband."

'They all on 'em looked at each other. "Now there's a challenge!" says youngest, and they all spit and shook hands on it. Off they goes home, all on 'em, to take another look at their husbands and see what they had to work with.

'Now youngest's husband was a bit dandified. Fancied hisself. Put his trousers under the mattress every night, to keep their crease, and if ever he copped sight of his reflection – in a mirror, a pond or a spoon – he whipped out his comb from his pocket and combed the long hair from the sides of his head over his bald spot. When the wind was blowing, he put his hand on his head, to keep his hair down. And if ever there was a young wench within half a mile on him, he near suffocated with holding his belly in.

'So youngest sister, her starts to spin wool into thread. Her husband had seen her spinning often enough, but this time her's spinning with empty spindle. He sees her spinning away for hours, but the spindle's still empty. He

101

wondered what was going on, but he said nothing, thinking his wife knowed what her was doing. And her did!

'Then he sees that her's set up her loom, and her's weaving, and working hard – but there's nothing on the loom, no threads, no cloth. So he can't keep quiet no more and he says, "What'cha doing, me love?"

' "Making you a new suit," her says.

' "Oh – that's nice," he says, and he squints at the loom, but he still can't see no cloth.

'His missis smooths her hand down where the cloth should be, and says, "Aint it fine? Madge was in here this morning, and y'know, her couldn't see it at all? But her always was common. Coarse. Can't appreciate the best. Sacking's good enough for her, and her lot."

' "Oh," says her husband, and clears his throat. "Beautiful," he says. "I've never seen you do better."

' "Thanks, love," her says, and kisses his cheek. "I can't wait to see you dressed in it. You'll look so handsome."

'Well, he thought he was handsome an' all, so he grins and nods and he takes another look at the loom; and he starts to think he can see summat. "I like that green fleck in it," he says.

' "I thought you would," says his missis. "It brings out the colour of your eyes."

'Now the middle sister, her couldn't think how her was to make a fool of her husband, as he was a quiet sort. But one morning, he happened to be singing to hisself. He didn't sing much, a'cos he had a terrible voice that

102

flattened every note flatter than a cow-pat. His wife had growed used to it over the years, but all of a sudden her heard it again, like the first time, and it near give her a headache. "Oh, sing that again!" her said. "I do love to hear you sing. You've got such a lovely tenor."

'Well, he starts laughing, thinking her was having him on, but he sung louder, to carry on the joke. "Oh beautiful," her says, and that night her says to him again, "Sing to me. Sing me summat sweet and gentle."

' "No, you sing," he says. "I bellock like a bullock."

' "No, no," her says, "there aint a better voice than yourn in the whole county."

'He laughs and says, "You'm the only one as thinks so!"

' "Oh, everybody else is jealous," her says. "That's why they throw clods at you when you start singing. Jealous of your beautiful tenor. Sing to me."

'Well, after a bit, her talks him into it, and he starts singing. Her had to keep thinking of the amber necklace and how all the beads shone like honey droplets – it was the only way her could stand it.

'But every morning, every night, her went on at her husband to sing for her, and her'd close her eyes, swooning-like, and kept after him about it so much that he started to believe he really did have a beautiful singing voice, and that all his life folk had just been jealous on him, and that only his wife – his loving wife – only her told him the truth.

'So he started singing everywhere, every day, no matter who was about; and if anybody groaned or begged him to shut up, he give a knowing smile and a wink, and went on singing anyroad.

'And at night he serenaded his wife in bed, and her gritted her teeth and clutched the sheets and thought: I'll have *earned* that necklace.

'The eldest daughter, her already knowed how her was going to make a fool on her husband. Long afore they'd got married, he'd done everything her told him to do, and if her forgot to tell him what to do, he come and asked her. He asked her what shirt he should put on in the morning, and whether it was cold enough to wear his nightshirt at night. If her asked him what he wanted for his dinner, he said, "Whatever you've a mind to make, dear."

'So, as soon as they got home from the funeral, her told him he was sick.

' "I don't feel sick," he says.

' "Oh, you look it," her says. "You look proper poorly bad. Go and get into bed and maybe you'll be better in the morning."

'So he did as her said, 'cos he always did, and her come and rubbed his chest with embrocation, and tucked him in, and went and made him a cup of hot milk. He lies in bed, drinking it, and thinks, "I must be sick, if her's making this much fuss on me."

'But in the morning he felt fine, and he come down-stairs for his breakfast. "What are you doing out of bed?" his missis shouts. "You'm never thinking of going out to work in your state of health!"

104

' "There's nothing wrong with me," he says.

' "You'm all pale and peaky," her says. "Back up them stairs and into bed, and don't even think of going to work afore next week."

'So he turns round and goes back to bed, 'cos his wife was a good, clever, sensible woman and he always does what her tells him. And her brought him hot-water bottle, and then later on some soup, and then a nice, cooling drink for his fever. And he lies there thinking, "Well, I feel all right, but her wouldn't be running up and down the stairs like this if I wasn't really bad." And he did start to feel a bit off-colour.

'Then the neighbours started coming in to visit him, and he felt worse, 'cos folk only come to visit you like that when you'm really sick. And his missis started feeding him on nothing but little bowls of thin porridge, saying he couldn't manage owt else – and there's nothing like living on porridge for making you feel bad.

'One day, towards the end of the week, when he felt like he could ate a couple of hosses, his missis come up the stairs to ask if he wanted owt. "Ar!" he says. "Get we a good big thick doorstep of bread and some of that ham you've got hanging in the chimney."

' "Oh, I can't give you that," her says.

' "Why not?"

' "I'm keeping that for the funeral."

'And then he did feel proper poorly bad.

'Couple of days later he felt worse, 'cos two big lads

carries a coffin into his bedroom. He sits up in bed and shouts, "What you bringing that thing in here for?"

'His missis come in behind 'em and says, "Lie down and be quiet. You'm dead."

' "I aint!"

' "You am," his missis says. "Would I have spent all this on a coffin if you wasn't dead?"

'That struck him, 'cos his wife was a sensible woman and a good housekeeper. "I don't feel dead," he says.

' "How would you know?" her says. "You've never been dead afore."

'That's true,' he says; and he lay down, and kept quiet while the two big lads puts him in the coffin. "Don't put the lid on," his missis says. Her has 'em carry the coffin downstairs and put it on the table in the kitchen, and when they'd done that, her paid 'em and sent 'em away. Her'd had the coffin brought from another town, so nobody else should know about it.

'The eldest sister stands by the coffin and says to her husband, "Now the neighbours am coming in to pay their last respects. You just remember you'm dead and don't go showing me up."

'So her husband got hisself comfortable and all the while the neighbours stood round the coffin, and ate his ham in sandwiches and drunk tea and gossiped, he kept still and quiet.

'Time come to set off for church, and the coffin's lid was put on. There was a little glass window in the lid, so they could still see the dead man's face. Everybody thought that was elegant.

'Six of the neighbours carried the coffin along the road. All along the way, the dead man kept thinking, "I don't think much to this coffin. There's cold draughts blowing right up the whole of the afternoon. I never thought I should still feel the cold when I was dead. It's a funny old life." 'Course, his missis had made sure there was plenty of air-holes in the coffin.

'They gets to the church, and it's only a little place, and there's so many folk crowded into it, that the coffin had to be propped up on its end by the altar, there being no room to lay it flat. So there was the dead man, staring out at his funeral through his little window, thinking, "It's nice to see such a good turn-out." And there's all his neighbours looking back at him as he lies in his coffin, saying to each other, "Now he's lost a few pounds, he's never looked better in his life."

'Then, down the aisle comes the youngest sister, arm in arm with her husband, the dandy, who's strutting along like the proudest cock in the farmyard, with his hair smoothed over his bald patch and his belly sucked in – and the only button on it his own belly-button, 'cos he's wearing the brand new suit his wife made for him.

'Everybody else stares at him as he comes to his pew, with everything swinging in the breeze. Everybody stares, and then starts to snigger, and then they put their hands over their mouths and keep quiet, 'cos they'm in church.

107

' "What a beautiful suit he's wearing," some whisper. They've been talking to the youngest sister. "It's so fine. Some folk can't see it, y'know." And when that gets round, the sniggering stops, and everybody starts admiring the green fleck that brings out the colour of his – something or other.

'Well, the dandy struts down to the front pew with his wife, and sits down by the second sister and her husband, and the widow. The man in the coffin's looking out through his window, and he thinks, "What's me brother-in-law think he's doing, coming to me funeral with not a stitch on and everything hanging out? No respect!"

'Anyway, the service goes on, and when they gets to the hymn, the middle sister's husband stands up by his starkers brother-in-law, and he starts to sing. He brays like a donkey, screeches like a gleed under a door, like an iron spoon dragged across an iron pan; he blares like a fog-horn. And all the time off-key and flat as a cow-pat.

'When they heard his noise the folk nearest him stopped singing – and then the folk further off could hear the din, and they stopped singing – and then even the folk at the back could hear this banshee howling and hullaballooing, and they stopped. Then there was nobody singing except the middle sister's husband. And *he* thought everybody else had stopped because his voice was so beautiful that they just wanted to harken to him, so he sung even louder.

'The man in the coffin looked out at his one brother-in-law standing there starkers, and his other brother-in-law bellocking like a constipated bullock, and he shouts out, "Even if I am dead, I shall have to laugh!" And he laughed so hard the lid of the coffin fell off.

'The church was empty afore the coffin lid hit the floor. The loudest yell – off-key and flat – was from the middle sister's husband; and the one to run away fastest – leaping over tombstones with everything swinging in the breeze – was the youngest sister's dandy.

'And running after 'em come the eldest sister's husband, shouting, "I'm sorry, come on back! Finish the funeral – don't mind me, I'm dead!" And funny thing, they only run the harder.

'But when it had all calmed down everybody agreed that the eldest sister had won the amber necklace.

'So, brothers – make sure you marry a clever woman, and make sure you never do what her tells you.'

People were still laughing at the story when Heaven's Door was thrown open and there, in the doorway, stood a recording Angel with a great book and a pen, to check the names of those wishing to enter, and, beside the Angel, St Peter, with his keys.

'I'm sorry to keep you all waiting,' St Peter said. 'Really, I do apologise, but we couldn't open the door earlier, we were so busy.'

'Doing what?' an old woman said. 'There's no work in Heaven, is there? I hope there's no work in Heaven. I've done enough of that on Earth.'

'We weren't working,' St Peter said. 'We were. Ah. Celebrating.'

There were angry exclamations, and shouts. 'Celebrating! While we were standing out here, you were celebrating!'

The Angel paused in its work of checking the names, and said, 'You don't understand. All the Blessed were gathered, to celebrate, to sing praise and rejoice at the entering into Heaven of a rich man.'

This made the crowd even angrier.

'Should have knowed better! One law for the poor, another for the rich!'

'I thought Heaven would be different!'

'Nobody's celebrating our arrival, I notice!'

The Angel said, 'You don't understand.'

'We understand!' many people shouted.

'You sing and rejoice for the rich, but not for the poor!'

The Angel said, 'Each time we open Heaven's Door, many, many poor people enter in, as now, and we welcome them. But when we open Heaven's Door to a rich man, then we rejoice! – for it happens only once in a thousand years.'

Then all the people fell quiet.

'Name?' said the Angel.

'Josiah Lamb.'

'Yes,' said the Angel, making a mark in its book. 'Enter. Name?'

'Algernon Grimsby.'

'Yes. Enter.'

And Mr Grimsby entered into Heaven.

## Nine

# Mary's Story

Heaven has many mansions, and the Sergeant went one
way, and Mr Grimsby another. Mr Grimsby wandered
alone through one mansion after another. Heaven is not a
crowded place. 'Hello. Is anyone there?'

He found no one and saw no one, until he pushed at a
door that was standing ajar, and looked in, and there was a
woman in a blue dress, standing at a table with a teapot in
her hand.

'Hello sweetheart,' she said. 'I'm just having a cup of
tea. Want a cup?'

'Yes, thank you, I will,' said Mr Grimsby, and went in.
She sat down, and he sat down, and she passed him a plate
of cakes. 'Excuse me,' he said, 'but haven't I seen you
somewhere before?'

'I'm sure you have,' she said. 'Sugar and milk, love?'

'Aren't you – aren't you – I'm sorry, I don't know what
to call you.'

'Just call me Mary, sweetheart. And what do I call you?'

'Me? Oh – Algernon.' And he blushed.

'Algy.' She put a cup in front of him. 'Don't let it go cold, Algy.'

'But, Mary, aren't you—?'

'I'm His mother, yes. And you, Algy, what did you do?'

'What did I do? Well, once upon a time, I managed a little business, a little brewery, you know – but that seems a long time ago, a long time. Latterly, I've been collecting stories . . . I did collect stories . . . I meant to publish them, but . . .' He looked about at the cloud-built walls of the room they sat in, and through the window at the stars. 'I won't be doing that now.'

'Stories?' said the Virgin. 'You collected stories?'

'From all sorts of people. Housemaids and old soldiers and – dying women . . .' He looked about him again.

'I used to love listening to a good story,' the Virgin said, pushing the plate of cakes a little closer to him.

'Oh? Do you know any?'

'Do I know any? I could tell you seven times seven stories.'

'It would be an enormous honour to hear just one from you,' said Mr Grimsby.

'There's no need to lay it on so thick, sweetheart – but would you like to hear one? Really? Oh well . . .' And the Virgin took a sip of tea. 'Listen,' she said—

'Once on a time, when pigs drank wine, and monkeys chewed tobacco, when hens took snuff to make 'em tough, and nothing seemed to matter, there was a poor man out of work. His name was Tom. He'd gone everywhere looking for work, but couldn't find any. He did what he could – pawned or sold everything he owned – and in the end he just had to beg on the streets. It was better than starving. He was standing in the street one day with his hand out, when along comes his old gaffer, the man who sacked him, walking with the Vicar.

'This gaffer was as rich as a king, but as mean as they come. He was so mean, when he killed a pig he saved its fart to blow its bladder up, then sold it for a football. Tom sees him and thinks, "There's a man who owes me a bob or two—" because he'd always been a cheating old swine, this gaffer. Fined the men if they was a minute late, made 'em pay to have their tools sharpened – he'd get 'em to work overtime and then he'd say, "You can choose. Will you be paid for your overtime, or have the sack?" So when Tom sees the old gaffer with the Vicar, he thinks now's the time to get some of that money back.

'So he goes up to his old gaffer and says, "Can you spare me a penny, Master?"

'Now, whenever anybody asked this old swine to give them money, it gave him a pain, just like a stomach-ache. So he screwed up his face and he's just going to tell Tom to go to Hell, when he remembers he's with the Vicar. Well, he doesn't want to show himself up in front of the Vicar, so he starts feeling in his pockets, as if he's going to give Tom some money, but then he says, "A penny? No, I can't give you a penny—" He's feeling through all his pockets, in his trousers, his jacket, his waistcoat . . . "I can't give you a penny. I've got no small change."

' "Threepence'll do," Tom said.

' "I've got no small change, I tell you."

' "Sixpence," says Tom.

' "I've got no small change."

' "And neither have I," says the Vicar.

' "I wouldn't mind a shilling," says Tom.

' "LOOK!" says the old swine, and then he remembers the Vicar. "I've got no small change now, my man," he says, "but come to my house in half an hour's time, and I'll give you a penny then." And he gets away at a good trot, arm in arm with the Vicar.

'And Tom thinks, "You aren't getting away with *that*, me old flower, you needn't think it." And he goes round to the old gaffer's house.

'He knocks on the door, and the gaffer's wife answers. Her doesn't like seeing this scruffy beggar on her step. "What do you want?" her says.

' "Sorry to bother you, Missis," says Tom, "but the gaffer told me to come here and he'd give me a penny."

' "Stay there," her says, and shuts the door on him, and goes to her old man and tells him, "There's a beggar outside, says you said you'd give him a penny. Shall I give him one?"

'His face all screws up and he says, "Give him nothing!"

' "But he says that you said —"

' "I know, I know! But give him nothing."

' "But he's waiting," her says.

' "Well," says the old swine, "tell him I've gone out."

'So her goes back to the door and tells Tom, "He's gone out; sorry."

'But Tom had been expecting this. "I'll wait," he says, and sits himself down on the doorstep.

'Back to the old swine goes the missis. "He's waiting on the doorstep," her says. "Do something. The neighbours'll see him, the dirty object."

' "Let him wait," says the old man. So they let him wait. But Tom was stubborn. He sits there all day. He goes off to find himself a bit of bread, but he comes back and sits there until it's dark. And he curls up and sleeps on the doorstep, and the next morning, he's still there, waiting.

' "Do something," says the missis to her old man.

'So the old swine says, "Go and tell him I've died. That'll get rid of him."

'So her goes out and says to Tom, "It's no use your waiting there – me husband's died."

' "Oh, I'm sorry to hear that," says Tom. "Was it sudden?"

' "Just this minute," her says.

' "Well, that's very sad," says Tom. "You'll be needing some help with making the arrangements?"

' "Oh no – I can manage."

' "Would you like me to lay him out?" Tom asks.

' "Oh no, no, don't trouble."

' "No trouble, seeing as I'm here."

' "You're too kind," her says.

115

' "Not at all," he says.

' "I can do it."

' "But I insist."

'And with a step this way and a step that, Tom's through the door and in the house.

' "Where is the old – gentleman?" he says, shoving open doors.

'The old swine of a gaffer only just has time to lie hisself down on the floor afore Tom barges into the room. Tom kneels down by him and takes off his hat respectfully – and the old swine has to hold his breath and do his best to look dead. Tom touches his hand. "He's still warm!"

' "I told you he'd only just died," the missis says.

' "Well, we'll wash him," says Tom. "Where's the kitchen? I'll get some water." And he's off to find the kitchen, with the missis tagging after, and her's saying, "Oh don't bother!" and he's saying, "Just being neighbourly."

'And the old gaffer, he's lying on the floor, not daring to move in case Tom comes back unexpected.

'Back Tom comes with a jug full of water out of the pump, icy cold water. The missis is still trailing behind him, bleating, "There's no need!" and "I can manage, honest!" Tom pulls open the old man's clothes and sloshes the cold water all over him. The old man tries to keep still, but it's such a shock he can't help but jerk about a bit.

' "He's alive!" Tom says.

' "Oh no," says the missis. "That's only the body jerking, the way they do."

' "Tell you what," says Tom. "I'll give him a shave, make him look respectable. He can't meet his Maker like that."

' "Oh, you're much too kind," says the missis.

' "Only being Christian. I'll use me own razor. It's a bit past its best, but it won't matter to the old un, will it?" And he takes out of his pocket a razor that's all blunt and nicked. And with the last of the cold water, he starts shaving the old man. He nicks him and grazes him, and makes his face as sore as a boil, but the old man won't complain, or twitch, because he doesn't want to give Tom a penny. He lies there as stiff as a board.

' "He keeps twitching," says Tom. "Are you sure he's dead?"

' "Oh, as a doornail," her says. "I'm sure he's shaved enough now."

' "Oh, we'll leave him smooth as a baby's bum," says Tom, and he keeps scraping away. Then he says, "You'll be needing a coffin."

' "Oh, you mustn't trouble."

' "No trouble. You'll be wanting a good coffin, for a rich man like him. I'll just nip along and get you one. Won't be long. Might be back any minute."

'And off goes Tom. 'Course, the old man can't move. He don't know when Tom might come back. So he's lying there muttering at his missis through clenched teeth. "What did you want to let him in for?"

' "I couldn't keep him out."

' "What am I going to do?"

' "Get up," her says.

' "How can I get up when he's coming back with a coffin?"

'And back come Tom with the best coffin in the coffin-maker's shop, a great big thing of polished oak with brass handles. Some men have come with him to carry it, and they lift the old man up, put him in the coffin and close the lid – and the missis is standing there, watching, and her don't know what to do or say for the best.

' "Carry him along to the chapel," says Tom to the men. "I'll follow on, and stay with the coffin and pray for him. D'you want to come, Missis?'

' "Oh no, I'm too overcome," her says, and drops into a chair. "I'll stay here."

'So Tom goes along to the chapel, and he sits in a pew close by the coffin, and he waits.

'The old man's lying in the coffin, thinking, "Has he gone yet?" But every now and again Tom calls out a bit of a prayer to let the old man know he's still there. And the old man thinks, "He's got to go sooner or later. I've stuck it out this far. I'll stick it out to the finish. Once he goes to get something to eat, I'll get out, and when he comes back he'll never know that I'm not still in here."

'But Tom was just as determined to stick it out, even

though it was getting dark in the chapel and cold. Tom was getting hungry, but he thought, "I'll stop here until the old swine has to come out and admit he was trying to cheat me, if it kills me." So there they both are, one in a coffin and one in a pew.

'But what neither of 'em knowed was that robbers used to come to that chapel, it being out of the way, to share out their loot – and when it was full dark, in they come, a rough lot, arguing and shoving each other. Lucky for Tom it was so dark, they didn't see him before he heard them, and he got down and hid under the pew.

'The robbers come up the aisle and they sat theirselves down just by the coffin. They didn't take no notice of it – it was just somebody's coffin to them. They started emptying their pockets and their bags and their boots – everywhere they'd got loot stashed – and they started sharing it out. They was quarrelling all the time – "That's mine" – "it baint" – "you've got that, I want this" – "you can't have it," and on and on like that. In the end they got everything shared out except for one thing – a sword.

'They all wanted this sword. "It's no good," says one robber, "it's blunt." But he only said that because he wanted to keep it, and he was trying to put the others off it.

' "It's well sharp," says another.

' "No, it's blunt, it wouldn't cut soft butter."

'Now Tom had been listening to all this, and now he spoke up from his hiding place. "If you want to see how

119

sharp it is," he says, "why don't you try cutting the head off the man in the coffin?"

' "All the robbers thought it was another robber that had spoken, and they all thought it was a good idea. Up they jumped, shouting, "Right! We'll see if it can cut the dead un's head off!"

'Well, the old gaffer in the coffin, he'd put up with a lot, but that was enough, and he ups and shoves open the coffin lid, shouting, "You baint cutting no rotten head off nobody!"

'And the robbers all went, "Aaaaargh!" and run out of the chapel and down the street, and never come there again.

'Tom got up from behind the pew and he says to his old gaffer, "You're feeling better, then?"

'The old man didn't bat an eyelid. "Never mind that," he says. "Look what we've got here."

'And what they had was all the robbers' loot piled on the floor.

' "It's mine," says the gaffer, " 'cos I scared 'em off."

' "It's *mine*," says Tom, "because you wouldn't have been here to scare 'em off if it hadn't been for me."

' "Don't I know it," says the gaffer. "I suppose we'd better share it then." Because the gaffer had seen how far Tom would go to win an argument.

'So they sat down on the cold stone floor and they shared everything out between 'em. The old gaffer knowed the price of everything, and Tom was no fool, so they managed to settle up between 'em even over things like the sword, and watches and brooches. And when they'd got everything sorted out, and they were having a bit of a rest, with their pockets and their boots filled with silver coins and gold coins and jewels, Tom all of a sudden says, "What about that penny you promised me, you stingy old so-and-so?"

'And the gaffer, with diamond necklaces hanging off his ears, and gold snuff-boxes in either hand, sitting in heaps of gold sovereigns, he says, "I keep telling you, I've got no small change!" '

And Mary, Christ's mother, laughed so you could see her back teeth. ' "I've got no small change!" Aint that just like some people, though? That's a good un, isn't it? Our Jesus told us that one.'

Mr Grimsby laughed too. 'A very good one, madam – but I'm a little surprised—'

'At what?'

'At your telling such a story. Surely – surely the robbers' loot should have been returned to the people from whom it was stolen?'

'Oh man,' said Mary. 'You'd spoil the story for that? Fill your face with cake and stop worriting.'

She watched him take a cake, and then pointed at him and said, 'I went in the garden to pick a bit of thyme – I've told my tale, now thee tell thine.'

'Oh – must I?' said Mr Grimsby.

'Don't you know any?'

'Oh . . . I must know dozens . . . But collecting them isn't the same as telling them, you know.'

'Well, I've told one, and now I feel like hearing one,' said Mary.

And who can refuse Mary, Queen of Heaven?

# Ten

# Mr Grimsby's Story

Mr Grimsby said to the Virgin, 'It's very hard to think of a story at a moment's notice . . . Oh, but I have one! This was a story I often heard my dear wife telling to our children when they were small. It's called, "The Dog Who Told Lies."

'There was once a forester who lived far from anyone in the middle of a wood. Every day he went off among the trees with his three sons, and his wife was left at home, all alone, to keep house.

'She was lonely, spending every day all by herself, and when her husband and sons did come home, they hadn't much to say for themselves. Often the poor woman was so lonely she would talk to her pots and pans and her own finger-ends.

'One day she was weeding her vegetable garden when out of the woods came a small dog who trotted over to her and sat down. "Hello," she said. "Where have you come from?"

' "Nowhere in particular," said the dog, "but I was

hoping you might let me stay here."

' "You can talk!" said the woman.

' "What of it?" said the dog. "By the way, you're pulling up a carrot."

'Well, the woman and the dog fell to talking, and they told each other all about themselves, and exchanged views on this and that, and the woman enjoyed their chat so much that she said, "I'd be glad to have you stay here! I can give you a warm place by the fire and plenty to eat, though it won't be fancy."

' "Thank you," said the dog. "I'll stay, but on one condition."

' "What's that?"

' "That you don't tell your boys that I can talk. You can tell your old man, but not your boys."

'Well, the woman had been looking forward to doing exactly that and she was disappointed. "Why not?"

' "Because I don't like boys," the dog said. "They're nasty and rough. They throw stones at one and tie cans to one's tail, and are thoroughly objectionable."

' "My boys aren't like that," the woman said. "They're good lads."

' "If you don't promise, I shan't stay," said the dog. And the woman wanted someone to talk to so much that she promised.

'So when the husband and his sons came home that night, there was the little dog lying on the hearth. "Oh, where did he come from?" said the sons, and tried to stroke and pat the dog, but it got up in a very cold and pointed manner, and hid among the woman's skirts.

' "I'm going to keep him," said the woman. "I like his company."

' "He's not very friendly," said her husband; but he changed his mind later, when his sons had all gone to bed, for then the little dog began to talk. It was well-informed politically, and had some interesting views on forestry, and the husband greatly enjoyed their chat, but at the end of the evening the dog said, "Well, I'm sorry, but I must ask you not to mention to your sons that I can talk. I have nothing to say to them."

' "I don't keep secrets from my boys," said the man.

' "Then I shall leave in the morning," said the dog.

'The woman begged her husband to keep just this one secret from his sons, because she was so lonely all by herself, and in the end the man agreed.

'So the woman enjoyed the company of the little dog all day. It followed her about as she did her chores, and they talked about everything, and grew better friends every day. But, as soon as the sons came home with their father in the evening, the little dog lay down on the hearth with its nose on its paws and made not a sound; nor would it allow them to pat it, or have anything to do with them. Once the sons had gone to bed, though, the dog would perk up and ask the forester about his day, and they would talk and argue like old friends.

'Then it happened that the household ran out of

necessities. That evening the woman asked her eldest son if he would walk into town the next day, and buy groceries. "Of course," he said.

' "And I was wondering, would you take my little dog along with you, to let him stretch his legs?"

' "Of course," said the son.

' "Mind you look after him, though. You know how much I think of him," said the woman. And the son said that he would.

'So, the next day, the eldest son set off for town, with the little dog walking beside him, on a lead made from a bit of string. The eldest son made sure that he didn't walk too fast for the dog's stubby little legs; and when it began to pant, he stopped and let it rest; and stopped again to let it drink from a stream. For he was a good-hearted young man, and he knew the little dog meant a lot to his mother; so he looked after it for her sake.

'When they reached the town, the son tied the dog to a fence, but he made sure it was on the shady side of the street, so it wouldn't be too fatigued by the heat. And on their way home, he stopped again to let the dog drink from the stream.

' "Did you take care of my little dog?" his mother asked, when they reached home.

' "Of course," he said.

'But that night, when the sons had gone to bed, the little dog lay on the hearth and moaned. "What's the matter?" the forester asked.

' "Oh," said the dog. "I didn't know people could be so cruel."

' "What do you mean?" asked the woman.

' "Your son dragged me along on that bit of string until I was half-choked, and he never let me stop for a rest nor a drop of water, though my tongue was dragging on the road. And when we reached town, he tied me up in the sun, with the traffic rattling by, until I was half-roasted and scared out of my wits. And then he dragged me home on the end of the string again, and I don't think I shall ever recover." And the dog sobbed piteously.

'The man and woman were enraged. The forester jumped up and shouted for his eldest son. "Come here at once!" he cried. All three of the sons came sleepily down-stairs, to see what was the matter. "Is this how you take care of your mother's pet?" the father shouted, pointing to the little dog shivering on the hearth. "I never thought a son of mine would be so cruel!"

' "How could you, how could you, when I asked you to take care of him?" the mother wept.

'The eldest son was astonished, and hadn't a word to say for himself. He couldn't imagine who had told these lies about him. His brothers were astonished too, but since they had been with their father, they didn't know whether their brother had mistreated the little dog or not – though it seemed unlike him.

' "Out of my house!" shouted the father at last. "I never want to lay eyes on you again!"

'And then the eldest son was angry and said, "I shall go! I've no wish to stay where I'm thought of so little!" And at first light he packed up his few clothes and left his father's house.

'Now life went on much as before for a while, with the two remaining sons working with their father, though they missed their brother. The father missed him too, but kept that to himself.

'The mother kept house, and talked to the little dog about how disappointed she was with her eldest son. "I tried to bring him up to be a good boy. I never would have thought he could treat you like that."

' "Never mind," said the little dog. "The best of mothers can often have the worst of sons, no blame to her."

'And the woman cried and told the dog how much she missed her son, despite his bad behaviour, and how sorry she was that they'd parted on bad terms.

' "Never mind," said the little dog. "You still have the other two. And you have me."

'In the evening, when the two remaining sons were in bed, the little dog talked things over with their father. "Maybe I spared the rod and spoiled the child," the forester said, of his eldest son. "But he always seemed to be such a good lad."

' "Well, many a father before you has come to grief by being too tender-hearted," said the little dog. "Never mind. Be stricter with the other two, that's my advice."

' "Maybe you're right," said the forester; and he was glad he had the little dog to share his problems.

'But then they ran out of flour again, and the woman asked the second son if he would walk into town and fetch some. "And I'd like you to take my little dog along for the walk too. And mind you look after him well, not like your brother!"

' "I will," said the second son, and, remembering what had happened to his older brother, he walked very slowly, so the dog had plenty of time to sniff at things along the road, and raise its leg, and generally take its ease. When they reached the town, he not only found a sheltered spot for it to wait for him, but bought it a platter of scraps from the butcher's shop, and set a dish of water for it. And on the way home, though he already had a heavy sack of flour to carry, he managed to carry the little dog under one arm too, so it wouldn't be tired.

'But that night, when the two sons had gone to bed, the little dog lay on the hearth and it sobbed and whined.

' "Whatever's the matter?" the woman cried. "Do you have a pain?"

' "I ache all over," sobbed the dog. "Every inch of the way to town, that wicked son of yours dragged me until I was half-throttled, and when I choked, he kicked me with his big boots until I don't think I have a hair that isn't growing from a bruise. And when we got to town, I was tired out, and my mouth as dry as chalk, but he tied me up in the sun and left me without food or water while he was in the pub drinking with his friends. And then he dragged and kicked me all the way home, and I think I might die."

'Well, you can imagine how furious the man and woman were. They both jumped up and yelled for their sons, and when the two sleepy boys came down, they shouted at the second son: "How could you be so cruel? After the way your brother disappointed us, how could you treat our poor little dog so badly?"

' "Who says I treated it badly?" said the second son.

' "Ah, you didn't think you'd be found out, did you?" shouted the father. "Well, you have been, and you can pack your bags and take yourself off. I won't have you under my roof another day!"

' "I'll go tonight!" said the second son, who had a temper as quick as his parents'; and he went back upstairs and packed his clothes, and set off into the night.

'So now there was only the youngest son left at home. And he was very, very good. At night, when he was in bed, the little dog told the man and woman that it was sorry for their loss. "I thought a lot of that second boy," said the dog. "He was the best of the three of them in many ways. I never would have believed myself that he would treat me as badly as he did. But there you are."

' "I blame myself," said the father. "I should have been stricter."

' "Oh, don't blame yourself for being kind," said the little dog, climbing on his lap to be stroked. "It's a sad thing, but some people are just born wicked."

' "Our youngest is still with us anyway," said the woman. "And he's a gem."

' "Oh yes," said the little dog. "He's a nice lad."

'Then came the day when the woman asked her youngest son to walk into town and buy some flour.

' "You don't want me to take the dog along, do you?" the boy asked nervously.

' "He needs the walk," said the woman. "And I know you'll look after him. You will take care of him, won't you?"

'The boy looked at the dog, which was looking at him. "I'll do my best," he said.

'The boy was so anxious to take good care of the dog that he carried him all the way to town, and never let him set paw to the ground. When they reached the town, he took the dog into an inn, and bought it a meat pie and half a pint of best bitter, and he left it to enjoy its meal while he went and bought the flour.

'On their way home, the boy couldn't carry the dog, because he wasn't as strong as his older brothers, and he had the flour to hump along, but he let the dog trot along at its own pace. About half-way, the boy stopped for a rest, and he took biscuits from his pocket and gave them to the dog, to keep its strength up. While the boy rested, the dog ran off into the woods, chasing rabbits; and when they went on again, while the boy trudged along under the load of the sack, the dog frisked and played by the road-side.

'That night, when the youngest boy was in bed, the dog began to whimper and sob. "Oh no!" said the woman. "Don't tell me my baby mistreated you, because I shan't believe you!"

' "Oh don't believe me then!" sobbed the dog. "Don't believe how he cut a stick from the hedge as soon as we were out of sight, and beat and kicked me every inch of the way along the road! And called me every wicked name he could lay his tongue to! Don't believe how, when we got to town, he tied me to the market cross, and got his friends to throw stones at me, and laughed every time I was hit! Don't believe me when I tell you that he never gave me a drop to drink nor a bite to eat nor ever a minute to rest. Don't believe how he kicked me all the way home! Don't believe me! And when you find me cold, stiff and dead tomorrow morning because of his ill treatment, don't believe that either!"

'Oh, the man and woman were furious! Up the stairs they went and dragged their youngest out of bed, and dressed him down and upbraided him, while the poor lad couldn't find a word. And they threw him out of the house and threw his clothes after him.

'In the morning they were sorry, and missed their youngest son more than the others. "It's sad, it's very sad," said the little dog. "I'm as grieved as you are, and my heart breaks for your trouble – but he was a bad lot, I'm afraid. A devil in a cherub's form. Never mind, never mind: you have me. I shall never leave you."

'The next time the flour ran out, there was no one to send to buy more but the forester himself. And, of course, he took his little dog along with him for the walk. He strolled into town, whistling, with the little dog trotting beside him happily, running off to sniff at this and that, drinking from the stream, fetching sticks.

'When they got to town, the forester went to the inn for his dinner, and he had a dish of water set for his little dog, and bought it a biscuit and fed it some scraps from his plate. Then, with the dog running at his heels, he bought the flour and started home.

'That evening he sat by the fire as usual, chatting with his wife and the dog. But then he had to go outside; and on his way back, he was passing by the window of the house, and he heard the little dog talking to his wife inside. And the dog was saying, "He beat me, he kicked me, he called me names every step of the way. He gave me salt-water to drink and laughed when it made me sick – and he gave me chicken bones to eat! And he kicked and thrashed me every inch of the way home."

'The forester went back into the house and said, "Oh you liar! Wife, this dog is a liar! I never hit or kicked it even once! I never called it names. I gave it biscuits and clean water for its meal and shared my own food with it!"

'The dog crept close to the woman, with its ears back and its tail down. Looking up at her, it said, "I'm not a liar. He was cruel to me!"

' "Wife, who do you believe – me or the dog?" the

forester asked. "I give you my word, I did nothing to harm it."

' "Oh!" said the woman. "Do you think it was lying about our sons?"

'The man looked at the dog. "Were you?"

' "No," said the dog. "I was telling the truth about them, I swear. They were cruel, wicked, rough boys."

'The man and the woman looked at each other, and they remembered how surprised they'd been that their sons would be so cruel. And the end of it was, they threw the dog out of the house, and told it never to come back.

'The forester and his wife were lonely and sad after that. Both of them often cried, to think that they'd believed the dog before their sons, and now they might never see their sons again. And they even missed the lying little dog, for when it hadn't been making mischief, it had been excellent company.

'The little dog himself went wandering along the roads, with his head hanging and his tail between his legs. The stones were hard to his paws, and he often did have to go a long way with nothing to eat and drink. He came on boys who did throw stones at him and hit him with sticks. When night came, he had to sleep in ditches or in open fields, and he was wet and cold and missed his warm fireside.

'At length, in his wanderings, he came to the edge of a marl-hole — that's a great hole from which marl, or clay, has been dug. They always have a pool at the bottom because they hold all the rainwater. Well, the little dog was wandering round the marl-hole, wishing he had something to eat, and that he wasn't so cold and wet, and that he had somewhere warm to sleep that night, when he slipped on the muddy ground at the marl-hole's edge, and fell into the pool at the bottom.

'Well, of course, he doggie-paddled to the edge, but when he tried to climb out, he couldn't, because the sides were too steep, and the clay too slippy. And the more he tried, the more his little paws became coated with wet clay, and the slippier they became. The more he struggled, the more he tired, and soon he began to sink in the water. He bobbed up again, but he was tiring fast, and knew he would drown. How he barked and shouted for help!

'Now three young men came to the edge of the marl-hole, to see what all the noise was about – and who were these three young men? They were the forester's three sons. After being thrown out of their home, they'd met up again, and had stuck together, helping each other out.

' "It's a dog shouting for help!" said the youngest.

' "A dog that can talk?" said the middle brother.

' "It looks just like our mother's dog," said the eldest.

'And then they all three looked at each other and said, together, "So *that's* who told those lies about us!"

' "Let's leave it to drown," said the youngest brother.

' "Serve it right," said the middle brother.

'But the eldest brother said, "No, that wouldn't be right. Besides," he said, squeezing the neck of his youngest brother, "it's only a little pup. Maybe it didn't know any better."

'So they ran to brick-works nearby – there's usually a brick-works by a marl-hole – and they borrowed a long rope. They ran back to the marl-hole, and tied the rope round the waist of the youngest brother, and then his two bigger brothers lowered him down the side of the marl-hole. The little dog swam to him, and he picked it up, and his two big brothers hauled him to the top again.

'The little dog shook itself and sent water flying everywhere. "Thank you," it said, and hung its head and its tail. "I'm sorry I told lies about you."

' "We don't want your 'sorries' or your thanks," said the eldest brother. "They're no use to us. I think you should go back to our mother and father, and tell *them* that you lied."

' "They already know," said the little dog. "They threw me out, and they wish they had you back."

' "Well, then," said the eldest brother. "Let's all go home together."

'So the three brothers all went home, and the little dog trotted at their heels for some of the way, or was carried in their arms when it was tired.

'No words of mine can tell how happy the forester and his wife were when they opened their door and saw all three of their sons standing outside. They dragged them inside, and wished for longer arms and more mouths, so they could hug and kiss all three of them at once. But they weren't so pleased to see the little dog.

' "You're the cause of all the trouble, you nasty lying little hound," said the woman. "Be off with you and don't come back!"

' "Yes, be off," said the forester, "before I really give you a kick."

'The little dog, its tail between its legs, turned to go.

' "If we can forgive it, you should," said the eldest son. "It was you who believed its lies, after all."

' "Believed it before your own sons," said the middle son.

' "Yes, forgive it," said the youngest. "I bet it'll never tell lies again."

'The forester and his wife were ashamed, and they called back the little dog and forgave it, and all of them lived happily ever after – and if the little dog ever told lies after that, it made sure they couldn't be found out.'

The Virgin laughed at the story, and said, 'I like that little dog, wicked little thing though it was.'

'I never understood, myself, why it told such outrageous lies,' said Mr Grimsby.

'That's easy,' said the Virgin. 'It wanted the mother all to itself, like many a naughty child. Don't I know!'

'It was my wife's favourite story,' Mr Grimsby said. 'So often I've heard her tell it to our little ones – and they loved it too.'

'It was *a* favourite story,' said Mrs Grimsby, who'd been

standing in the doorway, listening. 'But not my favourite.' She came in, stooped over her husband and kissed him. 'I'll tell you my *favourite* story,' she said, pulling out a chair . . .

And so she did. But if I set down the story of everyone who has a story to tell, then this book would never end, which it must, and it ends here.